THE
FREEDOM
CHAIN

THE
FREEDOM
CHAIN

SHAWN D. SMITH

AMBASSADOR INTERNATIONAL
GREENVILLE, SOUTH CAROLINA & BELFAST, NORTHERN IRELAND

www.ambassador-international.com

THE FREEDOM CHAIN

© 2024 by Shawn D. Smith
All rights reserved

ISBN: 978-1-64960-520-7
eISBN: 978-1-64960-562-7

Scripture quotations taken from The King James Version of the Bible. Public Domain.

Research for this book acquired from *History of the Christian Church* by Philip Schaff (Peabody: Hendrickson Publishers, Inc., 2006).

Cover Design by Karen Slayne
Cover Art and Illustrations by Raymon Mallari
Interior Typesetting by Dentelle Design
Edited by Katie Cruice Smith

Ambassador International titles may be purchased in bulk for education, business, fundraising, or sales promotional use. For information, please email sales@emeraldhouse.com.

AMBASSADOR INTERNATIONAL	AMBASSADOR BOOKS
Emerald House	The Mount
411 University Ridge, Suite B14	2 Woodstock Link
Greenville, SC 29601	Belfast, BT6 8DD
United States	Northern Ireland, United Kingdom
www.ambassador-international.com	www.ambassadormedia.co.uk

The colophon is a trademark of Ambassador, a Christian publishing company.

A Note to the Reader

During our homeschool study of ancient Rome, our family read several letters from Gaius Plinius Caecilius Secundus, known as Pliny the Younger. Nearly 250 of his letters have survived, including his correspondence with Trajan, the emperor of Rome. These letters provide a beautiful picture of ancient Roman life at its height. Nearly all of my descriptions of Pliny in this story—from his puzzlement with Christianity to the menu items he served Marius and Helena—come directly from his many writings. Schaff's *History of the Church* describes Pliny as a Roman "gentleman of high culture and noble instincts" that "ignorantly despised Christianity . . . while [serving as] Proconsul in Asia."[1] The word "ignorant" neither describes his educational status nor reverts to name-calling. Rather, it describes a man who, in his own words, did not know or understand the

---

1 Philip Schaff, *History of the Christian Church* (Peabody: Hendrickson Publishers, Inc., 2006), 796.

tenets of Christianity and struggled to comprehend the belief in only one true, all-powerful God. The Christian way of life perplexed him, and, unfortunately, he persecuted its innocent professors.

In studying Pliny, we discovered a man who loved learning. He considered it both a great privilege and an important responsibility to serve the people. He recognized that much had been given to him, and he spent his life attempting to use those gifts to make his world a better place. He fought for many social reforms, including better treatment of slaves. But as far as history records, he never found the One Who would give his life true meaning, and in reading his many letters, one can sense his quest for Truth.

One letter stood out to us. It was written to the emperor Trajan and describes the capture, investigation, and torture of two Christian deaconesses. Pliny showed devoted respect for Trajan and clearly loved him. He wisely sought advice from his superior about a problem he did not understand. He expressed an earnest desire to fulfill his duties to the utmost of his ability, yet it is sad to realize that this otherwise noble man was so far from the Truth that could have set him free. And although we cannot know the fate of the two deaconesses discussed in the letter, we do see that Pliny did not know what to do with them after he interrogated and tortured them. He tells Trajan that he "postponed my examination and immediately consulted you."[2]

As we read of the deaconesses, we wondered about them. We found ourselves imagining what life for those early Christians must have been like. We read some pretty tough stories of martyrs in order to learn more. A particularly powerful narrative was *The Passion of Perpetua and Felicity*, which I have added to the list of suggested reading at the end of this novel. I attempted to capture the essence of the Roman prison experience based on several accounts of the barbarous treatment many in the empire faced for their beliefs. Perpetua's account of her prison experience moved me more than any other. The details in her diary mirror everything we know about Roman prisons, and I depended heavily upon her writing to craft some of the painful prison scenes our two deaconesses endured in the pages of this novel.

It appears from Pliny's letters that, at least in Bythinia, many Christians had been taken, questioned, and executed. I developed the fictional story, *The Freedom Chain*, very loosely based on the story of the

---

2 William Stearns Davis, *Readings in Ancient History* (Boston: Allyn & Bacon, 1913), 221.

two deaconesses discussed in Pliny's letter. Trajan did eventually respond to Pliny regarding the trial of Christians. He told him not to seek them out and not to consider anonymous accusations. However, if the accused were guilty of being a Christian, then they should be punished. Interestingly, Trajan never described the punishment, although he did affirm Pliny's handling of the two women. Pliny died after only two years as proconsul in Bythinia (about the time of the setting of our story), so we have no record of whatever happened to the deaconesses. As far as we know, he never placed his faith and trust in Jesus Christ alone for his salvation. He never knew the peace he spent his whole life pursuing.

It is my desire that as you read this story, you will find comfort, courage, and mercy from the blessed hope that is in Jesus Christ.

GLOSSARY OF HELPFUL TERMS

In writing a story based on a former time period, it is difficult to be faithful to terms and expressions that are so foreign to our current vocabulary. In an effort to bridge the gap from ancient Rome to the twenty-first century, I have sparingly used certain Latin and modern terms interchangeably. My hope is that it gives you, the reader, a feel for the ancient era without crippling readability.

BASILICA: A basilica was a building used for many public services, such as courts of law, banking, commercial offices, and even shops.

BITHYNIA: This province was in northwest Asia Minor, and its northern border was the Black Sea. The biblical book of I Peter was written to "the strangers scattered throughout Pontus, Galatia, Cappadocia, Asia, and Bithynia" (1 Peter 1:1).

DOMINUS: This term literally means "lord" and is used in much the same way that an English servant would address his master. Throughout this story, I have used it interchangeably with "lord" or "my lord" to help with readability while still providing the feel of ancient Roman culture.

EMPORIUM: This large building or warehouse was usually on or near the shores of a main port. It was used to maintain offices and store goods.

GOVERNOR: The word "governor" is an English term and is often used to describe one of many Roman offices. In this book, I have used it, again for readability, as an interchangeable term for Pliny's role as proconsul.

ICHTHUS: This was a secret "code word" developed by early Christians to help them identify one another. Ichthus was the Greek word for fish, and the acrostic meant I—Iesus (Jesus), CH—(Christ), TH—Theou (of God), U—uios (Son), and S—Soter (Savior). Therefore, a Christian would often mention Ichthus to another in hopes of determining whether he was speaking to a brother or sister in Christ. It is quite possible that our modern symbol of the fish (representing Jesus) derives from this well-known secret password of the Early Church.

LEGIONARY: This term is sometimes changed in modern writings to "legionnaire," but I have chosen to use the original term to describe a soldier of the Roman legion. Also, since "legionnaire" is associated with the French Forcign Legion, I hope to avoid confusion.

MANUMISSION: This was the act of freeing a slave. If the master was a Roman citizen, then the freed slave automatically became a Roman citizen.

PERISTYLE: A garden or courtyard, usually enclosed, that was often surrounded by a colonnade. This was a common feature in Roman homes.

PROCONSUL: To understand the power of a proconsul, one must first understand the role of the consul, the highest Roman magistrate. Only two consuls were elected each year, and their rule extended throughout the empire. A consul was elected for one year. The title proconsul was given to a consul, usually after his year of service was complete. Proconsuls most often ruled a province, but sometimes, they had military commands. In this story, Pliny served as proconsul of the province of Bithynia. He was clearly a highly respected and accomplished man.

TRICLINIUM: This term refers to a Roman dining room.

TUNIC/TUNICA: Nearly all ancient Greek and Roman people wore some form of a tunic/tunica. Its basic form consisted of a rectangular shape with simple holes for the head and arms. It was belted or tied with a cord and was usually longer in the front than the back.

CHAPTER ONE

Ten-year old Cassia couldn't remember the first time Mistress Helena struck her, but she did remember running from the room screaming for her mother. Her mistress often masked her strikingly beautiful face with ugly, snarled fury; and in recent months, that fury, combined with excessive amounts of strong drink, often resulted in physical attacks. Cassia seemed to be the one who bore Helena's wrath most often during those moments; and the spiteful words, combined with the beatings, pierced the young child's soul.

Mistress Helena called for Cassia shortly after the evening meal. Cassia entered the bedchamber with her head bowed, but she still noticed the utter shambles all around her. Her hands clung to the tattered ends of the rope that tied her tunica at her waist. She nervously twisted the rope between her fingers while staring at the colorful mosaic tile floor. Mistress Helena slunk toward Cassia and ordered her to remove pieces of a hand-painted urn smashed against the wall during a moment of rage. Helena's porcelain hands held a near-empty flask of wine, and her body tottered tipsily as she approached the young slave.

"Clean up this mess, girl," she ordered, slurring her speech slightly.

"Yes, my lady," Cassia replied. She quickly retrieved the broom from the corner of the room and began her work in earnest. She dared to glance at her mistress and noted the vacant eyes and the way her mistress wobbled as she moved toward the bed. Cassia always feared her mistress' wine-induced tempers.

Keeping one eye on her mistress and one eye on her work, Cassia began sweeping the broken pieces into a pile. Mistress Helena pointed to an array of necklaces, tunicas, and shawls strewn about the room.

"When you are finished there, you can put away my things," she demanded, her arm sweeping the room. Her golden bracelets bangled against each other and echoed off the stone walls of the bedchamber with soft, tinkling tones. Cassia noted that the pleasant sound was a sharp contrast to the state of her mistress' volatile mood.

Cassia bowed in humble obedience and replied, "Yes, my lady." She found a container and swept the pile of sharp fragments into it; then she dutifully picked up the first tunica from the floor. She carefully folded the smooth fabric and wistfully admired the

expensive garment. She glanced away from her work to check on Mistress Helena and suddenly cut her finger on a piece of the exquisite, broken pottery that had found its way into the folds of fabric.

She jerked back slightly, and a single drop of blood landed on the brightly tiled, mosaic floor. The movement caught Mistress Helena by surprise, and she spilled some wine on her hand. She hurled her goblet across the room and erupted. Her normally cultured voice tightened; and an angry flush colored her smooth, pale skin.

"Cassia, come here at once," she said, her eyes blazing and her body reeling.

"Y-yes, m-my lady." Cassia stood, cowering, and moved to within inches of her mistress. The first blow knocked Cassia backward, and she tumbled to the ground.

"I'm . . . I'm s-s-sorry, Mistress," she uttered, tears welling into her eyes. "Please . . . "

Her mistress towered over her and struck her again, her gold ring tearing through the skin below her eye. "You stupid girl. You are an imbecile. I'll teach you to carry out your duties." Her speech slurred like a hissing snake. Cassia threw up her arms to shield her face, crouching against the torrent of what was to come.

Mistress Helena unleashed blow after wild blow on the poor child's frail body, screaming abuse with every one. "You *will* put away my clothes, and if you so much as leave a dribble of your rubbish blood or dirt on them, you will pay with your life. You are nothing but worthless chattel, you filthy imp."

Cassia had no idea how many times she was hit. Thankfully, her mistress was intoxicated, and many of her blows either missed altogether or were so weak, they barely hurt. Cassia had been able to block most of them with her arms, but she struggled to scramble away from the barrage.

After a particularly harsh blow landed on her upper cheek, Cassia heard Titus' commanding voice. "Stop!"

Titus was the overseer of all of Master Marius' affairs. When the master was gone, Titus ruled the household with such authority that not even Mistress Helena usually dared to cross him. The moment he spoke, Cassia felt intense and hopeful relief. She knew she would be safe for the remainder of the evening.

Mistress Helena froze, her hand poised to strike mid-air. Her breaths came in short, desperate heaves as she stood straddling Cassia. She glanced at Titus, then back at Cassia.

Titus approached and commanded again, "Stop." He grabbed Mistress Helena's arm and forced her to turn and face him. "Enough, Mistress! Enough." He pulled her away from Cassia and forced her toward the door.

"Come with me, Mistress." As he led her out of the room, Phinneus, the head household slave, rushed to Cassia's side. He helped her sit up and clutched her awkwardly as he knelt beside her.

"Your mother is on her way," he soothed. "Let's see if we can get you up."

Cassia shuddered, closing her eyes and hugging her knees. She tried to take deep breaths but could only manage shaky, shallow gasps. Tears cascaded down her cheeks one tiny droplet at a time from her red-rimmed eyes, creating a slow but steady stream. As the salty moisture reached the cut on her cheek, she winced and gently patted the welt that was forming just below her eye. She traced the open cut with her fingertips, then wiped at her tears to keep them from stinging the wound.

Phinneus lifted her chin and tilted her swollen face to the side. "That's going to sting for a bit," he said, "but you're going to be okay." He patted her head awkwardly and helped her stand.

She noticed the garments still littering the room and dutifully reached for one. Phinneus took it from her hand. "Cassia, we'll finish the room. You are done tonight."

"But—" Cassia protested.

"I said you are done," Phinneus gently interrupted.

Cassia's mother, Livia, ran into the room, and Phinneus quickly moved toward the door. With a slight two-finger gesture, he beckoned to two other slaves who quietly entered and began straightening the room.

Mother wept while hugging her daughter. "Oh, Cassia, Cassia. I'm so sorry, my darling. I'm so very sorry." She wiped away the tears on Cassia's cheek and assessed the wound. "Come with me, darling. Let's get that cleaned up."

Mother tucked some loose strands of hair behind Cassia's ear. Her hand cupped her child's swollen face, her fingers resting just under the chin. She tilted Cassia's head so their eyes met. "It will get better, darling. Master Marius will be here any day now. He'll make everything better."

Cassia followed her mother down the long, open hallway toward the back of the villa. When they reached the narrow steps at the end, Mother stood back so that Cassia could begin the climb to their tiny room tucked under the eaves. She followed closely behind, keeping a hand on the small of Cassia's back. Once inside, Mother led Cassia to the small sleeping mat against the wall. While Cassia scooted onto the mat, her mother crossed the room and grabbed a small, linen cloth from a simple stone shelf carved into the wall. She dipped the cloth into a basin of water, and after wringing it out, she joined Cassia on the mat.

She barely touched the wound under Cassia's eye when Cassia crumbled into her mother's lap weeping. She gently turned Cassia's face toward her and bent down and kissed her swollen cheek. Her own tears mingled with Cassia's.

Cassia lay with her head in her mother's lap and cried while her mother gently cleaned the wound below her eye and wiped away each tear. "It will be okay. It's going to be okay," she soothed.

As Mother stroked her daughter's dark, curly hair away from her forehead and whispered words of encouragement, Cassia's tears eventually subsided enough for her to talk.

"Does it hurt very badly?" Mother asked.

"Not as much as it sometimes does," Cassia replied between hiccups of sorrow.

Mother slowly shifted Cassia off her lap while she got up and wrung out the cloth again. She also poured a drink for Cassia. "Drink this. It will help you catch your breath."

Cassia obeyed; and after a few swallows, her short, rapid breathing stabilized, and she could finally take some deeper breaths. Mother made her take a few more sips and then took the cup and set it on the mat next to them. She climbed back up next to Cassia.

"I'm so sorry I wasn't there for you, Cassia. I'm so, so sorry."

Mother searched her eyes then, and a flicker of distress crossed her face.

"Oh, Cassia, my darling, I see your hatred. Don't let the bitterness grow," she pleaded.

"I do hate her," Cassia replied vehemently. "I hate her so much, I should like to—"

"Hush, my sweet Cassia. You must remember Whom you serve."

Cassia's eyes filled with tears again. "Oh, Mother," she sobbed, "I do try. I try so hard to do as she asks. But I . . . I just can't please her, and she gets so angry." As she spoke, her voice became high-pitched and frenzied. "I find my fists tightening and my teeth clenching, and I want to hit back."

"Oh, my dear child," Mother whispered, running her fingers through Cassia's thick, black curls. "I know it is unjust, it is wrong in every way. But . . . we are slaves." Mother's eyes were wet, and she faltered.

She stared blankly at the stone wall behind the low bed they both shared.

"I wish Father were still here." Cassia voiced what they both were thinking. "He always made things better." New sobs overtook her. "I miss him so much, Mother. I'd take a thousand beatings if I could just have Father back. Why did he have to die?" Her voice broke, and she threw herself back into her mother's lap. Violent moans exploded from her frail body.

"Shhh, Cassia. Please don't cry." Mother's words were almost a whisper. She waited patiently for Cassia's sorrow to subside, and when it did, she lifted Cassia's face once again to her own.

"We must pray for Mistress Helena. What she does is wrong, but we are slaves. We have no privilege. But we do have hope. We have One Who fights for us even when we don't understand how."

Cassia closed her eyes, listening to Mother's gentle rebuke. "Jesus is the greatest Example of how we should deal with injustice, isn't He?" She rubbed Cassia's shoulder. "Remember how He prayed? He asked His Father to forgive the very men who were crucifying Him."

Cassia simply listened. She could not speak.

"When Mistress Helena becomes dangerous, you must escape and get help," Mother continued. "If I am not close by, Titus or Phinneus will rescue you. Other servants will protect you. Her behavior is unjust when she strikes you for no cause. But you must remember that we are still her slaves. We must serve her with a humble spirit, and we must release her to God and pray that she will find our Savior. That doesn't mean we excuse her behavior—what she does is wrong and should not be tolerated. But God is a God of perfect justice. He can be trusted. And just like the prophet Isaiah proclaims, He can make beauty from these horrible ashes."[3]

Mother was gentle, and despite how difficult her life had been, she remained faithful to God. Her eyes were always filled with peace, and her spirit was kind and good. Cassia knew Mother genuinely loved both Mistress Helena and Master Marius, and she served them with warmth and care. If only Master Marius was here. Things were always better when he was home. Mistress Helena drew great strength from her son.

As Mother spoke, a quiet confidence gave courage and hope to Cassia's troubled spirit. "Remember Peter's letter to us?"

Cassia barely nodded, and Mother continued, offering strength from the words of the apostle. "He wrote a part specifically for us slaves. Yes, you

---

3 Isaiah 61:3

suffered unjustly, but if you respond with the love of God, you go against the natural response. You may be the one who can show Mistress Helena the power of God—a power so great that it allows you to love her, despite the injustice she inflicts upon you. That kind of power is supernatural, and that is what will change her life."

Mother continued, "Mistress Helena needs the Savior, Cassia. She is so lonely, and she's searching for peace. Her body is wasting away from illness. And this is the time of year when she observes the losses of both her husband and her granddaughter." Cassia listened, but she subtly shook her head. She wanted to show sympathy to her mistress, but her heart rebelled against it.

Livia stroked Cassia's bruised cheek, and Cassia noticed another tiny tear escape down her mother's cheek as she continued almost in a whisper, "I wonder if Helena doesn't think of her granddaughter, little Julia, when she sees you. Did you know that you were both born on the same night?"

Cassia had heard bits and pieces of the story over the years, but it helped to hear it again when she was so angry at her mistress.

Mother recounted the events of so long ago. "It was a night of joy and sorrow all mixed together.

Everyone excitedly awaited the birth of little Julia. That sweet newborn would make Helena a grandmother and Marius a father for the very first time. No one expected Marius' wife to have such trouble with the birth, and when the doctor finally decided to take the baby . . . " Mother paused. A soft sob escaped, and new tears formed as she reverently related the memory. "Master Marius's sweet wife was too weak to recover from the trauma. She died that night, leaving him with his little daughter. After that, the whole household changed."

Mother was quiet then, and except for the occasional sniffle from Cassia, all was silent.

Cassia eventually shifted to a sitting position and leaned her head on her mother's shoulder. Mother wrapped her arm around Cassia's tiny frame and offered one more glimpse into Mistress Helena's soul. "That's why she drinks so much these days. She's so lonely, and broken, and just lost. She raised little Julia as her very own child. She loved her and cared for her with a gentle compassion that seems foreign now." Mother shifted to lean her back against the wall.

"I'm sorry, dear. I just want to remind you that our mistress was not always so angry. It wasn't so long ago that she made this household the liveliest and happiest home in the entire province. When she helped Master

Marius raise little Julia, she had never been happier. But then, just three years later, the fever took both her husband and little Julia. Helena's desperate sorrow changed her. Just by loving her, you may be able to lead her to God and the peace that He alone can bring."

Cassia shook her head. "I can't be the one to do it, Mother. I'm not strong enough."

"Oh, my darling, none of us are strong enough. It is a miracle of God, visible in our lives when we see His power accomplish things we cannot. You need to put yourself wholly in God's hands to become His instrument. Remember, you are not here to please yourself or Mistress Helena; you are here to please God. God is never pleased when you suffer because you have acted in a rebellious or sinful way. According to Peter's letter, what pleases God during suffering is when you suffer for doing good and still trust in Him. So, you must ask God to help you every day—no, every minute—to respond to your mistress in a holy way."

Mother sighed deeply. For several minutes, the two sat in comfortable silence. Eventually, Mother sat up a little straighter. "Let's get you to bed. It's been a long day, and tomorrow will be brighter."

Cassia scooted to the edge of the settee, and Mother dipped the cloth into the water basin again.

She gently wiped the wound on Cassia's face once more and then smiled. "You are beautiful; do you know that? I'm so thankful for you."

Cassia smiled, then winced a little. They both laughed, which caused Cassia to wince even more. "Don't make me laugh, Mother; it hurts."

"I'm sorry, darling. I don't mean to laugh."

Still, a few more giggles passed between them before Cassia stretched out onto her sleeping mat. Her mother covered her with a blanket and bent down to kiss Cassia's forehead.

"Mother, do you love Master Marius?"

Mother's eyes widened, and her lips parted slightly. The slightest shade of pink began coloring her cheeks. "Cassia, you know I love both Mistress Helena and Master Marius."

"No, Mother. I mean do you *love*-love Master Marius."

Mother's cheeks flamed, and she looked away from Cassia. "Why would you ask such a silly question, Cassia?"

Cassia simply replied, "Well, I know that you spent a lot of time with him just before he left on his last trip. And when you would come to bed at night, you would sing lots of happy songs. And sometimes, the dark brown of your eyes seemed to kind of sparkle. And if you married Master Marius, then we wouldn't be slaves anymore, and I wouldn't have to worry about Mistress Helena hitting me ever again."

Mother released a deep breath and leaned over to blow out the candle. "Hush, Cassia. Try to get some rest. Tomorrow will be a busy day."

"But do you love the master?"

Livia patted Cassia's head. "What you dream of is not possible, my child. Go to sleep now."

Cassia closed her eyes, and it only took a few minutes for the gentle noises of the night to lull her to sleep.

CHAPTER TWO

Livia squinted, waiting for her eyes to adjust to the predawn sky. She shook out her thick, black hair and scooped it into a simple twist at the nape of her neck. Then she tied it in place with a threadbare scarf and draped the edge of it over the crown of her head. She tiptoed around the edge of her sleeping mat and felt her way to the corner of the room.

Sliding her hand across the small, stone shelf, she found the flint and felt for the torn, linen fiber wick in the oil lamp. She struck the flint against a small, iron pyrite stone, and directed the resulting sparks toward the wick. A small ember began to smolder on the linen tinder, and she cupped her hand around the clay lamp and blew steadily on it. When the ember grew into a satisfying flame, Livia stared at the light dancing off the stone walls of their tiny room. She inhaled slowly, held her breath as long as she could, and then exhaled through her mouth, controlling the rate at which she released the air. The practice calmed her, and she stood watching the flickering light while deeply breathing in and out a few more times.

Holding the lamp, she turned around and knelt near Cassia. The puffy bluish-purple welt under Cassia's eye felt warm under Livia's fingertips. She tiptoed back to the low shelf, placing the lamp off to the side. She dipped the cloth into the small basin of water, added a few drops of oil to the worn fabric, and wrung it out over the basin.

She turned again to Cassia and smoothed back the soft, black curls that were so much like her own. The curls dangled across her child's forehead, and Livia found herself smoothing her own wisps of hair from her own forehead at the same time. She smiled realizing how similar they were, but her heart hurt for this innocent soul.

"Oh, Cassia," she whispered. "I'm so sorry."

She placed the cloth strip onto the wound and held her breath when Cassia stirred and let out a low moan. "Hush, my love. You are fine. Just rest." Cassia never fully awakened and easily drifted back into her slumber.

Livia climbed onto her mat and leaned against the wall with a sigh, staring at the flickering flame. Soon, the first rays of morning would begin to touch the fields of the villa where the sky and earth meet. She breathed another deep breath, savoring her favorite part of the day. She loved watching the first strands of color pierce through the blackness of the night and birth a new day.

A slight grin formed as she pondered Cassia's question. *Do you love Master Marius?* Livia's smile widened. *Of course, I don't love . . .*

She leaned her head against the wall, watching the way the light danced about the room. Each flicker brought an image to her mind of each happy moment she'd spent with the master before he'd left for his last trip—walks in the garden, discussions near the peristyle, glances and smiles when she saw him around the estate. She closed her eyes, and all she could see were the dark pools of his eyes with which he listened so intensely to her words.

Do I love Master Marius? I care deeply about his soul. I feel like we've built an unusual friendship.

Livia didn't have an answer—at least, not an honest one. After her husband had died, she never dreamed she'd love again. She was a slave. She did not have options. Her grief still consumed her at times.

But something had changed last year. The master saw her weeping and praying to God. He was also grieving, and he had questions—lots of questions. And sometime during the days, weeks, and months that followed, his questions had become different. They weren't all about the Holy Scriptures and the tenets of Christianity. Sometimes, they were about flowers—like what were her favorites. Sometimes, when the questions ran out, they just talked about their shared grief. And just before he left, they had begun talking about hopeful things for the future. He had told her about his business ventures, and she had often made him laugh telling about some of Cassia's adventures.

Livia admitted she felt happy when the master called for her. She admitted she felt almost free when they walked and talked together. She could even admit that she often longed for a glimpse of him throughout her day because just the sight of him often cheered her. But she could not love him because . . . loving him was not an option. She was a slave. He was not a Christian. She could not and would not give her heart away to someone who did not share the most important thing in her life.

Cassia stirred, and Livia stiffened. "Will the master be back today?" Cassia croaked, turning over with a yawn as she stretched her arms over her head.

Livia sat forward. "How are you feeling this morning, darling?"

Cassia tugged her blanket more closely around her shoulders and shivered a bit. "I'm okay, just a little sore." She drew her knees toward her chest as she lay on her side, and with her hands clasped under her chin, she sighed.

Livia grinned. "You know that your father used to call you a little praying babe when you slept like you are now."

"What do you mean?" Cassia asked.

"It's just that ever since you were a little baby, you would sleep in a little ball like you are now with your knees bent and your hands in front of you tucked under your chin, and he always thought you looked like you were praying. Sometimes, he would just sit and stare at you until you woke up."

"I like hearing stories about Father." Cassia rolled over onto her back and stretched her legs out. "Sometimes, I feel like I'm forgetting him."

Livia stood up and slowly rolled her neck from one shoulder, down toward her chest, and over to the other shoulder. She could hear the occasional cracking of her neck bones releasing the stiffness. She bent over Cassia and smoothed her hair back from her forehead.

"You don't have to worry about forgetting him, darling. You may change how you remember him. You may not always be able to picture him exactly as he was, or you may not always remember every detail of his face; but you will always remember how he loved you. You will always remember you had a father who cherished you completely."

Livia watched Cassia's smile grow. She reached a hand toward her daughter. "How about we start our day? I do believe that Master Marius could be here today. Phinneus told me yesterday that you will need to go into town this morning and make sure Brother Justin has his cart ready. You'll also need to go to the market and bring home a basket of his favorite fruit."

Cassia yawned again and grimaced as she tenderly fingered the wound below her eye. She grabbed her mother's outstretched hand and stood to her feet. "If the master is coming home, then today is going to be a wonderful day."

Livia smiled. She felt the same way. She helped Cassia dress and walked with her down to the garden and through the archway near the front of the villa. The slightest glint of light reflected off the pool near the gate, and a couple of birds chirped a hearty "good morning" as they passed beneath their nest. Livia hugged Cassia before sending her on her errand to town. "Be careful, and hurry home. The master could be here soon."

Cassia bounded out of the gate, and Livia, still grinning, turned back to the villa. Suddenly, she stopped. Perched on the gate sat a dove—not just any dove but *the* dove. The grayish pink feathers and distinctive black collar etched into its neck were unmistakable. "No," she whispered. Why this bird? Why today? She shuddered as a chill of premonition overtook her.

She glanced at the sky; this was supposed to be the best part of her day. The Creator's paintbrush was awakening His world with sparkles of sunshine beginning to glisten on the dewy blades of grass. But she no longer saw the sunrise. Instead, she pictured the flashes of soldiers' blades as they entered the villa. She saw her husband's face as they bound his hands and led him away. She looked at the dove again. Its red-black eyes seemed to hold her gaze with an ominous warning. She felt like running. "Should I run, little bird? Is that why you are here?" Her voice was barely a whisper.

"It's just like before," she heaved, panting for breath. Her hands trembled as she reached for the latch of the gate. She closed her eyes and remembered every brutal moment when, two years before, she had met this same dove on a morning just like this one. And on that morning, everything had changed forever.

When she shook the gate, the dove flew away, and Livia forced herself to take several deep, controlled breaths. She kept trying to swallow, but she couldn't. She put a hand to her chest to push back against the insane beating she felt just below her skin. *It's just a bird, nothing more.* Over and over, she told herself it was just a silly bird. The trauma of that day so long ago had not pushed its way to the surface with such force in more than a year. But that bird perched on the gate exactly like he was the day the soldiers had come at precisely the same time of the morning triggered the same terror she had felt the day they had taken her husband from her.

Cassia could tell the day would be warm, not hot. The meadow grasses rippled in rhythm with the wind like the waves on the sea below them. Noisy gulls bawled above the water, circling their prey. Cassia looked up and down the dusty road. It was still solitary at such an early hour, though far to her left, nearly on the horizon, a few slaves bent over, tending the massive gardens of their masters. She lifted her ragged tunica, stained and frayed from the nature of her labor, then carefully climbed over the grassy knoll and down the gritty bank to the rocky shore below.

A wisp of unruly, black hair blew across her wide, dark eyes and dusted her gaunt face. The sea welcomed her to its lonely coast, and she remained still for many moments, breathing in the salty air. This forlorn patch of earth was her haven.

Down the shore, several seagulls tore into some hapless creature, and she envied them. She realized that she had not grabbed her typical morning slice of bread and fruit, and on cue, her stomach made a loud protest. She patted her belly and inwardly promised to feed it as soon as she returned to the villa.

She wedged her basket between two rocks, then bent down and removed her worn leather sandals. She glanced up at the road again, making sure she was still alone, then tiptoed to the water's edge. She lifted her tunica into a wad, draping the material on her left arm, then let the waves trickle over her bare feet. She stood motionless for many minutes, allowing the breeze to cool her cheek.

Eventually, she lifted her hand tentatively to assess the damage. Just below her right eye, the skin was still hot and swollen. The slightest pressure of her fingers made her wince.

She bent down rather indelicately and splashed the cool water onto her face. Though the water refreshed her wound, the salty spray stung. She didn't care. Most of her body ached. She knelt there, splashing handful after handful of water onto her bruised face until her movements seemed frantic. Most of her hair and the front of her tunica were dripping wet before she finally stopped.

When she did, her agony spilled out in a torrent of sobs. She stood slowly and returned to the rocks below the embankment. She sat against the largest boulder and drew her knees toward her chest, and with her head buried in her hands, she wept.

Cassia tried to erase the memory of her latest punishment, but the experience was too fresh and raw. She shuddered, closing her eyes, and hugging her knees even tighter. The memory of her mother's tears and broken heart brought fresh tears to Cassia as she sat by the sea. She could almost feel her mother's trembling hands as she had guided Cassia back to their room and gently cleaned and soothed her wound.

A seagull swooped down close to Cassia, rousing her from her thoughts. Cassia bowed her head and turned to her only source of strength. *Oh, Lord, I don't know how to love Mistress Helena. Please help me. Help me respond rightly. Help me work hard with a good spirit.*

Suddenly, she heard the faint sound of hooves beating the packed earth above her. She sat completely still, her eyes scanning the road. Puffs of dust indicated a large crowd, and a quick glance proved it was a troop of soldiers. She hoisted her damp tunica and rolled her body around to the backside of the boulder, pressing tightly against it and the clay overhang of the embankment. Her breath was heavy, and she closed her eyes, praying she hadn't been spotted.

Like the pitter-patter of soft rain, the sound grew. She waited, willing herself not to move when it became a thunderous roar as it rushed above her head. As quickly as it had come, it left, storming down the road toward its unknown destination in the Bithynian countryside.

When the soldiers were completely out of site, Cassia grabbed her sandals and fumbled to tie them quickly. She then grabbed at a root above her head and pulled herself up. Just as she reached the top of the bank, she threw her head back in disgust and lowered herself back to the rocks. She grabbed the forgotten basket and ascended the rocky slope once again.

This time, she ran down the dusty path, taking no notice whatsoever of the countryside that had filled her senses only half an hour before. She stumbled over the tentacles of a tree root forcing its way through the gravel road and sprawled ungraciously across the road tearing her tunica.

Fear spurred her quickly back to her feet. She left the road, crossing through an open pasture and cutting off a fair distance. She delicately breached the crumbling stone wall on the other side of the field and came within view of Nicomedia. She futilely tidied her wet garments, patted her hair, and walked into town.

CHAPTER THREE

Marius Luciano paced the deck wiping the sweat from his brow. One corner of his mouth was turned slightly upward, and he rubbed his hands together. His dark, piercing eyes widened as the shore came into view.

"We'll be anchored in a few minutes," a deckhand yelled.

Marius's grin widened. The moment he felt the jolt of the ship meeting the sand, he jumped into the shallow waters along the shoreline, splashing the salty spray onto his expensive robes with each step. When he reached the sandy beach, he shook out his garments and warmly greeted his most trusted servant, Titus, clasping both hands on the smaller man's forearms.

"Good day, Friend Titus. It is good to see you again."

"And you, Master Marius. I trust your trip was profitable." Titus bowed slightly to his master and waited for him to pass before quickly falling in step behind him.

All around them, the bustling racket of the wharf stifled further conversation. Merchants hollered orders to weary servants carrying crates and barrels of cargo. Fishermen sat in groups talking over the noise while they repaired their nets. Others, returning from their night at sea, unloaded their catch and yelled over the head-splitting din. Lively tidewater slapped into the many craft moored along the shore. The beach was littered with scurrying workers, each intent on their own tasks.

Marius and Titus reached a stony path and climbed up to the street above the beach. More noise welcomed them as carts and wagons, heavy-laden with merchandise, clambered along the thoroughfare toward the many ample emporiums that lined this section of the city. Marius breathed in the salty air of Nicomedia. He loved sailing, but he always loved coming home.

They cut through the crowds and crossed the main avenue, then turned sharply down a side alley. In minutes, they reached their destination, quickly ducked into the porticus, and crossed the rectangular courtyard to their own emporium offices.

Striding across the room, Titus reached for a flagon of freshly pressed grapes and quickly poured a refreshing drink for his master.

"Thank you, Titus. I am parched." Marius gulped the juice, then set the goblet on a wide table near the window, running his fingers through the stubborn waves of his thick, closely-cropped, black hair. Wiping the sweat from his weather-tanned brow, Master Marius quickly removed his outer cloak, revealing a travel-dingy, white tunic, held firmly in place by a gold-encrusted belt. With a sigh, he dropped below the window, resting on a cool, stone bench.

Titus moved to the far corner of the room and lifted the latch of a large, mahogany cabinet. He pulled the heavy door open and removed a freshly laundered, bright white tunic and some clean, dry sandals. He placed them across a nearby table, then retrieved a large basin and cloth. He knelt before Marius and was removing the old sandals when Marius spoke.

"How have we fared these months I have been away?" He sat back against the stone wall and closed his eyes as Titus expertly washed his feet and massaged fragrant oils onto his master's muscular calves.

Still intent on his work, Titus replied, "You will be pleased to know that we have had our two largest returns since my tenure as your overseer. Malchus returned last month with the finest silks I have yet seen, and I have already sold the entire load for more than double our investment. Lex sailed in three weeks ago with oils and spices from Greece and beautiful timber from Gaul. With your load of grain from Alexandria, our coffers are full."

He paused briefly while he reached for a dry cloth, then expertly dabbed the excess oil off each leg and foot. A small grin formed on his mouth, and he continued, "Surprisingly, after your mother chose her favorites, we still had enough left over to turn a sizeable profit."

Marius laughed heartily and slapped the bench. "I suspect Mother chose our finest selections of everything, didn't she?" His voice was jovial as he pictured his dear mother grabbing all the best wares for herself in order to block any of her aristocratic friends from bettering her.

"Aye, that she did, *Dominus*. That she did." Titus chuckled softly as he finished lacing the leather straps around Marius's leg. Titus stood and carried the heavy basin to the window. A quick glance below proved it safe to dump the slop without splattering any unsuspecting passersby, so he poured out the liquid and returned the basin to a low bench positioned just below the window.

Titus grabbed the fresh tunic and handed it to Marius, giving final guidance to his master. "I have placed fresh water in the inner chamber. When you are ready, we can review the inventory."

Marius swiftly rose, took the garment from Titus, and motioned for him to wait, then entered the inner chamber.

Once inside and alone, he paused to consider all that he owned. His father had left him a thriving business with contacts throughout the Mediterranean world. In the years since his father's death, Marius had expanded his family's influence, increased their trade routes, and significantly grown their wealth. He rubbed the expensive garment in his hands with satisfaction.

With a deep sigh, he walked over to the porcelain bowl and cupped some water in his hands, splashing the cool liquid onto his face. When the water settled, he placed his hands on each side of the basin and studied his reflection in it. He grinned, knowing that he was finally about to get the one thing—or rather, the one person—he most wanted. He could almost picture her lifting her shy eyes to his when he told her his news. And, then, suddenly, his brow furrowed, and the corners of his lips lowered. He closed his eyes and lowered his chin to his chest.

To his surprise, it was Aurelia's face that briefly flitted across his mind. A part of him still felt like

Aurelia was with him, and he wanted to tell her his news. The emotional jerk back to his wife still caught him off-guard every time it happened. His grief often confused him, and moments like this made no sense. It wasn't that he felt he was betraying Aurelia by allowing his heart to care for another woman; it was that he was sad he could not share with her the hope and joy he was experiencing. And yet, if she hadn't died, he would not be feeling such deep love for another. The emotional turmoil that grief played in his thoughts often tormented him, and the vicious cycle of happy and sad mixed together was hard.

For so long, Aureila had been his confidante, and she had been the one who understood the issues of his heart. She had been a good wife, and when she had died, he had thought the grief would overcome him. She had been young and beautiful and full of life. They both had loved their status and influence in the community, and Aurelia had thrived on entertaining the wealthy citizens of Nicomedia. She had loved participating in all the events that the aristocracy enjoyed, and even though Marius had to admit she was sometimes rather shallow, he also remembered fondly how much fun life with Aurelia had been. Her engaging personality had made it impossible for him to stay angry with her for very long.

He sighed. She had been so young. Back then, their lives had never been marred by difficulty. That was no longer the case for him. The scars of grief sometimes consumed him. He was changed, and he knew it.

Marius shook his head and grabbed a linen towel from the top of the table. He wiped his face and hands as if to wipe away the painful memories of Aurelia's untimely death. He reached for his tunic and started to change his clothing, while his thoughts continued racing.

Julia—his beautiful baby, Julia—was the reason he had survived the grief of losing Aurelia. Julia was a happy and bright child and had chubby, little fingers and round, rosy cheeks. She had brought sunshine to their home; and Marius, with his mother and father's help, had found the strength and courage to move on when Aurelia had died in childbirth. They all loved little Julia and doted on her to a fault. Closing his eyes now, he could almost hear her giggles when he tickled her little tummy.

The muscles in his throat suddenly constricted, and he felt as if he couldn't swallow. He slumped onto the cold, stone bench next to the table. The night his little Julia had died replayed in his head. A violent illness had overtaken her. She had become lethargic and weak, and he remembered how hot her skin had been. He remembered cradling her in his arms and feeling hopeless as he watched the life slip from her big, dark eyes. She had closed her eyes and nestled against his chest. Her breathing had become more and more labored, and then she had just drifted off. He remembered the silence that had surrounded him that night as he tried to hear her next breath. It never came. His child was gone.

Marius shook his head. The memory still haunted him, and he did not want to dwell on it anymore. He tried to take a deep breath, but his chest felt as if a crushing weight was pressed against it. He grimaced thinking about how, only three days after Julia's death, the same fever had taken his own father. Marius heaved, remembering how hopeless he had felt during those grief-filled days. He remembered how desperately he had needed his father to help him through the pain but how angry he had become knowing that his father was gone, too.

He remembered how he had escaped into his work. He had sailed with his crews nearly every opportunity he could. Each time he came home, he had wanted to comfort his mother. But he was restless, and it was hard to stay with her very long when her grief was so strong. Still, they had become each other's sole sources of hope.

Over the years, he had seen the toll the sorrow had taken on his dear mother, and he worked hard to spare her the pain he saw in her eyes. He stayed home more and tried to be strong for her. But no matter how hard he tried, neither of them could truly be comforted. His mother had become more hopeless, and Marius himself had become numb to life. Each day was just a series of activities that took him through the motions of living without any purpose or hope.

Marius opened his eyes and lifted his head to the ceiling. He straightened his shoulders, and with glistening eyes, he raised his hands, palms upward. "Thank You, God, for not giving up on me," he whispered. "Thank You for healing my wounded soul."

He lowered his arms, adjusted the belt on his tunic, and ran a hand through his hair again—a habit his mother often teased him about. Knowing that Titus was waiting for him, he stood to collect himself. His final thought as he headed toward the warehouse door was one of gratitude that God, in His mercy, had sent that one special person into his life to give him hope and healing—Livia. Livia had opened his eyes, and he could not wait to tell her that not only were her prayers for him answered, but also that they could finally be together.

With renewed energy, he returned to meet Titus. From his broad shoulders to his narrow waist, every inch of Marius Luciano bespoke affluence and privilege. Over the next hour, he sat with Titus and reviewed the company's accounts. In the next room, more servants began filing in, stacking the warehouse walls with the new cargo Marius had recently accumulated. He was pleased with the state of his affairs; and when he and Titus finally climbed into the carriage, he was at peace.

"I'm not sure even Father himself could have dreamed we would see this kind of success," Marius said.

Titus lifted his chin slightly toward his master as a genuine smile curved his lips.

When they reached the main square of Nicomedia, they stopped abruptly. With a quick nod from Marius, Titus exited the coach to determine the cause of their delay. Marius reached into his pouch and felt for the heavily jeweled necklace he had chosen for his mother. He hoped she would be pleased, and he hoped even more that it would help erase the anguished, empty look in her eyes.

He allowed his fingers to drop further into the pouch and stroke the other gold chain he had purchased. It was much simpler than the gaudy show he had purchased for his mother, but it was for a more delicate soul. Though it had been seven years since his little Julia was taken from him, he could not help commemorating each birthday with a small gift for Helena. He could see his mother now as he offered it to her. She would carefully remove last year's chain from her wrist and place it in her rose-colored, sandstone box. Then, she would lovingly rub it the way he rubbed it now before doubling it around her wrist, where it would stay for the rest of the year.

He leaned his head back against the crimson velvet of the coach, closed his eyes, and tried to picture the face of his dear child. She would be ten now, with thick, dark curls and beautiful, ebony eyes. He envisioned pudgy, rose cheeks and a dimpled smile. She would have had her mother's easy smile and happy spirit.

Just then, Titus climbed back inside to report, and Marius sat upright. "Soldiers are leading some prisoners to the palace. They are turning the corner as we speak, so we will be moving again shortly."

Marius nodded and leaned his head against the seat. "How is . . . how is my mother, really, Titus? Is she . . . has she changed any?" It seemed highly inappropriate to ask his overseer such a question, but he knew Titus well enough to know he would get an honest answer.

Titus, who almost never looked him straight in the eye, studied his master before replying. "It is hard for me to say, Master."

"Please, Titus. You may speak freely. I must know her . . ." Marius paused. After hesitating for a minute, he continued, "I must know her state of mind."

Titus glanced at his hands, which were folded in his lap. Silence filled the carriage for many moments. When he finally spoke, his words were deliberate, but he did not deny the painful truth. "Your mother struggles most at this time every year. She still mourns for your father and your daughter as if their deaths were fresh." He took a deep breath. "In the past, her sorrow was only in her eyes. Her lively laughter had vanished, and she became gloomy and taciturn. However, in recent months, she . . ." He paused again and glanced at Marius as if afraid.

"Please, Titus, continue. You need not fear my response."

"Well, in the last year, she has changed. She appears frail. She rarely leaves her bedchamber, and worse, she drinks herself into a daily stupor. Her behavior is erratic and volatile. Her temper leaves every servant treading lightly with fear of her retribution. The worst of it is that . . . " Titus dropped his head to stare at the floor as he continued. "She has . . . well, she has focused her wrath on an innocent . . . " Titus shook his head. "I should not speak thus to you, *Dominus*. Please forgive me. Just know that I believe her health is declining, and it is affecting her demeanor."

Marius frowned; his eyes narrowed thinly; and he tapped his fingers against his knees. His concern was evident, but he also struggled to envision his mother in such a drastically uncharacteristic state of mind. "Has she seen a physician?"

"Many times, *Dominus*. It just doesn't seem to help." Titus stared out the window, clearly trying to avoid the subject.

Marius tried to engage Titus further, but recognizing how uncomfortable he had become, Marius respected him enough to drop the matter. "Thank you for what you have shared. Perhaps it is time for me to stay home more to care for the needs of my household. I appreciate your honesty."

"If I may speak to the matter once more, my lord."

"Please, go ahead."

"When you are present, Mistress Helena is happier. The whole household functions better, and . . . and those who suffer most have a reprieve. I am glad you have returned."

"Thank you, Titus. I will consider what you have said." Marius paused and phrased his next words carefully. "I believe I have found the thing that will help my mother. If she accepts, it will change her life forever." Marius had not discussed his newfound faith with anyone, but he was confident that once his mother heard the truth, her restless heart would finally be at peace.

"Then, may we hope she accepts your offer, Master."

The rest of the ride was spent in comfortable silence. Marius wondered at Titus's words, but he believed that soon, all would be well. His mind instead centered on Livia. It was Livia who had first introduced him to Jesus Christ. Her gentle spirit had always impressed him, but it was her unshakable peace that had prodded him to question her further.

It was about two years previous, and her husband had recently been killed by the proconsul for refusing to recant his Christian faith. One night, a restless Marius had entered the topiary garden near the servant's quarters. There, to his amazement, Livia knelt praying to her unseen God. Marius had been strangely moved by the sight of this widowed slave who possessed such immeasurable peace. She had told him of the One Who comforted the comfortless and Who cared for the widows and fatherless. She told him of Jesus, Who offered the same gift to all people—Roman, Greek, barbarian, master, and slave alike. She had offered to introduce him to this great Savior, but he had refused then.

Over the months, though, he had studied her. No slave worked harder. No slave showed more respect, and no slave was more trusted. She was the only one who could calm Mother's troubled spirit. Something about her was different, and he found himself envying her, longing for what she had. He began to seek her out. Over time, he found himself looking for her throughout the day. They would walk together as she patiently answered his questions about God. Sometimes, he called for her when his grief overwhelmed him. She always came, and just her smile soothed his spirit.

They developed an unusual friendship. He believed she enjoyed their evening walks as much as he did, but they never really talked about it. Shortly before he had left for his most recent trip at sea, he knew their friendship had changed—at least for him. He loved Livia, and he knew that they could finally be together now that he had found Christ. He couldn't wait to tell her.

CHAPTER FOUR

The low mumble of town reached Cassia's ears as horses and carts scuttled to and fro. She entered the city and immediately left the main road, filing down the narrow streets off the main square. Along one wall, baskets hung low, jutting into the walkway. As short as she was, she still had to duck her head to avoid some of the larger displays. The opposite wall held beautifully woven rugs and delicate fabrics. Further down, the old potter's limestone wheel ground out a steady rhythm as colorful, decorated pots sat hardening around him.

At the carpenter's workshop, she turned down a nearly hidden alley just to the left of the main entrance. Ezra, the carpenter's son, put aside the winnowing fork he was fashioning and waved to her. Ezra was one of her dearest friends. He was a couple of years older, but for as long as she could remember, he had been part of her life. They spent almost all day together every Sunday, and though he was shy and awkward around most people, he relaxed whenever he was with Cassia.

"Good morning, Cass . . . " He stopped when he saw her face.

Cassia started to answer, but the thudding of Brother Justin's mallet muffled her voice. Ezra touched his father's arm, and he ceased his hammering long enough to turn around and welcome the girl.

"Good morning, young maiden. I suspect you are—Oh, Cassia, not again. Come, child."

He held out his arms and pulled her into a hug. Brother Justin was a big man, strong and sturdy. To people who did not know him, he could seem intimidating; but to Cassia, he was a gentle, kindhearted man who had become a father figure since her father's death.

After a long and tender hug, Brother Justin gently pushed her away from him and inspected the wound more carefully. Ezra brought her a ladleful of water, and she drank thirstily.

"Come, sit down and tell me about it." Brother Justin motioned to his old stool, and when she was seated, he knelt on one knee next to her. Ezra reached for a cloth and dipped it in the water, clumsily offering it to Cassia and waiting for her to speak.

She thanked him for his kindness and briefly told her tale. She recited the events while staring at the floor and absently twisting the rope of her tunica. She dared not look at either of them because she was close to tears, and her voice was quiet and low.

When she finished her story, neither Brother Justin nor Ezra spoke at first. The normally noisy carpenter shop was uncomfortably quiet. Then, Cassia heard Brother Justin's rich, quiet voice offering intercession on her behalf. She looked up then, and fresh tears spilled down her cheeks when she saw her big, burly friend humbly bowed before her. The fervency with which he prayed moved her more than any other words of comfort could. She dabbed her eyes with the cloth Ezra had given her and tried to pray with him.

When Brother Justin finished praying, his own eyes were glistening. He kissed her forehead and drew her close, smoothing her long, uncombed hair with his hand.

Cassia cleared her throat and glanced uneasily at her friends. "I really can't stay. Master Marius is expected soon, and Mistress Helena—"

"I know; I know. She wants the cart wheel I promised," Brother Justin interrupted. "You'll be pleased to know I've already finished it and taken it to Titus's berth. He has fitted the wheel and is already waiting at the docks. I saw Master Marius's ship this morning, so he may well be on his way home even as we speak."

As he stood, he smiled broadly and added, with a twinkle in his eye, "I would not want to disappoint your mistress, child. She frightens me."

Cassia could not help but smile. He was so much like her father, laughing often and easing others' burdens. Brother Justin clearly had nothing to fear from Mistress Helena. His broad shoulders and thick upper arms were no match for the petite, fragile frame of her mistress. When he stood and walked back to his worktable, Cassia smiled and quietly thanked God for these wonderful friends.

She loved Brother Justin. He was a deacon at the church and had been one of Father's dearest friends. When Father was killed by Governor Pliny, Brother Justin had risked his own life to save him. As a Roman citizen, Justin had privileges that gave him more freedom than most of their other friends. Furthermore, he had spent many faithful years as a legionary, and he knew many powerful people. Yet even he could not save Father from the cruel sentence of the proconsul. Many others in their congregation had met the same fate, their only crime being their commitment to Jesus Christ.

Cassia still remembered the awful day the soldiers had come for her father, and even now, she cringed whenever she saw soldiers. She shivered, then gathered her basket and stood.

Brother Justin leaned back and raised an eyebrow, puzzling at her clothing. "May I ask how you came to be so . . . wet?"

Cassia looked down at her tunica. Shame filled her eyes, and she unconsciously covered herself with her hands. "I . . . I stopped by the sea to splash water on my face. It felt good, and I guess I used too much."

Brother Justin threw his head back and laughed. "I guess you did. Ezra, why don't you take our friend upstairs to Mother and see if she can help?"

"Oh, no, sir, I really can't wait. I still have to go to the market, and if Master Marius is really on his way home, Mistress will want a grand feast prepared in his honor. I must hurry." Without waiting for a reply, she headed toward the door.

"Perhaps I could go with you. I have just finished this staff and must deliver it to Master Felix, and it is only a mile further to your estate," Brother Justin said. "Ezra, prepare my cart. When we return from the market, we'll take the cart the rest of the way. It will save us much time."

Cassia hoped he did not see the fresh tears well up in her eyes, and she quickly wiped them away. However, his furrowed brow and watery eyes indicated that he had not only seen her tears but also that he felt her pain.

Cassia smiled and tried to wait patiently while Brother Justin untied his apron and put away his tools. She glanced down the alley toward the main street and planned her trip to the market, trying to remember any shortcuts that could save her time

Brother Justin gave instructions to Ezra, then inspected the staff one last time. His rough hands glided over the smooth edges, and he seemed satisfied. "Well, then, shall we go?"

Cassia curtsied slightly to Ezra and handed him the tearstained cloth. He smiled shyly and simply replied, "God go with you, my friend."

"Thank you, Ezra." She smiled, then followed his father out the door.

They headed down the alley toward the main thoroughfare leading toward the docks. The crowds seemed noisier than usual, and she could hear loud laughter and jovial banter. Just as they reached the street, Cassia saw soldiers. She instinctively shrank back against the stone wall and waited behind Brother Justin.

The soldiers were getting closer, but she could not see them well. People lined the street now and taunted the poor souls being dragged along. *Oh, Lord, please don't let it be another one of our friends.* Cassia's prayer was silent, and she sensed that Brother Justin was praying the same thing.

A man in front of Cassia bent to pick up stones to hurl at the unsuspecting offenders, and Brother Justin gasped. "It's Sister Clio," he started; then his breath caught. "Oh, no. No, please, no!" He paled, and his voice broke.

It was then that Cassia got her first glimpse. She pushed away from the wall and peered between the shoulders of the thick crowd before her. Her stomach lurched as her eyes met those of her mother. She shrieked and lunged out from the alley.

"Mother, Mother!" she screamed. Her wrenching shrieks could barely be heard above the taunting crowd. Her mother shook her head, silently pleading for Cassia to stay back. But Cassia could not, and she pushed against the layers of people.

Suddenly, a strong arm encircled her, and a hand went over her mouth. It drew her back toward the alley. She kicked and tried to loosen the iron grip.

The arm did not give, and her eyes sought Mother's one final time. Mother was smiling and nodding her head. She seemed pleased with Cassia's plight. She mouthed, "I love you," then disappeared around the corner, headed straight for the proconsulate's palace.

Cassia fought against her assailant, dragging her feet, jerking her head, and writhing her body to get free. She saw the crowd begin to dissipate behind her, then realized it was Brother Justin who held her so firmly. They ducked into his workshop, then through the narrow door leading to their home.

She barely heard his animated shouts to Ezra. "Close the door," he ordered. "Get the shutters, too." Ezra obeyed immediately, while Cassia tried to push her feet against the wall. She heard the crash of the work table as it toppled over as she fought to get free. But Brother Justin's strength easily controlled her panicked body, and all her frantic fighting was in vain. When they were in the upper chamber, he began talking, but his hand was still firmly covering her mouth.

"Cassia, I will try to help your mother, but you must not scream. Do you understand me? We must not let them take us, too. I need to take you back to your home and inform Mistress Helena; then, I will get some help. Promise me you will not scream."

When she nodded, he slowly removed his hand from her mouth. She dove into his arms and sobbed.

Justin made no attempt to hush her tears but gently wrapped his big, strong arms around her, cradling her against his chest, stroking her hair, and patting her back. Cassia's body eventually relaxed against him, and he finally released her.

Cassia thought she was calmer, but when she finally looked up into Brother Justin's compassionate eyes, she collapsed and sobbed all over again. "Not Mother, oh, Lord, please don't take my mother." Over and over, she sobbed and prayed, and her torment muffled her voice against Brother Justin's chest. She knew Governor Pliny's intention, and she knew her mother would not deny her faith. Mother was going to die.

Brother Justin tried to console her, but he could not. He turned to Ezra and his wife, Jaalah, whose eyes were filled with questions. "We have much work to do. I need you to lock the shop and come back here."

Ezra immediately exited the room. Within minutes, he was back and quietly nodded to his father.

Cassia finally pulled away and sat mutely. Tears flowed down her puffy cheeks, and her swollen eyes barely acknowledged Brother Justin. Her only sound came in periodic bursts of anguished hiccups.

"Cassia, look at me."

She turned her sad eyes on him trying to focus through the pools of tears. A great spasm shook her entire frame as another gasp for breath overtook her.

"Do not leave this room. Ezra will stay with you." When she did not respond, he knelt beside her and lifted her chin. "Cassia, you must listen to me. Do not leave this room. I will return soon. Sister Jaalah is going to take care of you, and Ezra is here. Do not leave. Do you understand me?" She meekly nodded, and he hugged her close one more time.

After he left, Cassia fell across the table moaning and crying. Ezra stood behind her patting her back. Little prayers began in her soul. They were constant. They were simple, and they broke the heart of God. Sister Jaalah stroked Cassia's hair and tried to offer soothing words, but none came.

Chapter Five

Phinneus greeted Marius's carriage at the courtyard gate. "We're so glad you arrived safely, Master," the older slave stated, while his hands fidgeted uncharacteristically. When he reached to help Marius descend the steps of the carriage, he blurted out with utter impropriety, "I must speak with you at once." He bowed low before Marius and held the door as his master descended the steps of the coach.

"Thank you, Phinneus. We can speak soon, but I will see my mother first. Please have my things delivered to my room." He turned toward the arched gateway behind the luxurious fountain, then paused. "Oh, and please have a tray of fruit delivered as well."

"'Tis already done, my lord, but I really must speak with you." The old servant bowed again, seeming even more distressed.

"It can wait," Marius interrupted, already entering the courtyard.

"But, Master, it is important," the old slave urged as he fell in step with Marius.

"Phinneus, I said it can wait. I will attend to you soon." Marius waved his hand in dismissal and nodded to Titus to have him speak with Phinneus.

Marius heard Titus begin interceding with Phinneus and smiled. His life was good, and he was happy—truly happy. His step was light as he strode beneath the rose-covered trellis and inhaled its sweet scent. He found himself glancing through every archway, hoping for a glimpse of Livia, who had led him to his newfound peace.

Various servants greeted him with genuine joy as he strode through the peristyle and down the open corridor to the staircase leading to the inner rooms of his villa. He did not hear their hushed whispers after he passed them, and instead, he skipped up the steps, taking them two at a time.

He was just about to knock on the door of his mother's room when he heard a loud crash and undecipherable screaming. He rushed through the door, expecting to find serious injury, and was, instead, knocked backward by a ceramic vase hurled right at his chest.

He grabbed for the door frame, fighting to remain upright; but the unsuspecting blow overpowered him, and he went down.

His mother's screams changed to wailing as she rushed to her son, begging forgiveness. "Oh, Marius, my son, my son," she whined. "Please forgive me. Oh, Marius, I'm so sorry. Are you hurt, son?" Her desperation roused him, and he struggled to sit up.

"Mother, I am fine, but what—"

Before he could finish, she threw herself across his chest and wept bitterly. He patted her head and tried to comfort her, but her fit was too frenzied. He noticed Phinneus in the corridor and nodded. The servant bowed and began quietly barking orders to the slaves who were carrying Marius' belongings. Phinneus then quickly disappeared into Marius' room.

While Marius waited for his mother to calm, he studied the room. Broken pieces of pottery littered every corner. A beautiful porcelain pitcher lay shattered in a puddle of water near the marble-topped table beneath the window. The washbasin was cracked and leaking its contents slowly down the gold inlay of the Egyptian cabinet against the north wall. Jewelry was strewn about the bed and floor, and clothing was pulled from neat piles on the shelves and tossed carelessly about the room. Marius could have no better picture of his mother's emotional stability. Now, he understood why Titus was so hesitant to discuss her. Marius had no idea things had gotten so bad.

In his desperation, he silently turned to his newly discovered source of comfort and prayed. *Oh, Father, I am astonished. I do not know how to help her. Please help me, Lord. Help me show her Your peace. She needs You so much, Lord. Oh, Father.* His spirit wept. No more words came, but he knew his Lord knew the depth of his pain.

Phinneus returned and placed a large basin filled with cool water near Marius. A soft cloth was draped over the side of the basin. Marius nodded again, and the servant left without a word being exchanged. Marius shifted and upturned his mother's tear-stained face. He gently brushed the hair away from her eyes, then kissed her forehead.

"I'm here, Mother, and I am not going anywhere. Please, let me help you."

Fresh tears spilled down her puffy cheeks, and he gently began wiping them away with the cool cloth Phinneus had brought. "Come sit with me in my room, will you? Tell me what makes you hurt so much," he coaxed.

He moved her to the side and stood. Then, he offered his hand and practically lifted her to her feet. That's when he noticed how much frailer her frame had become since he was last home. He put his arm around her waist, leading her to his chamber; and he felt her relax against him, while tiny sobs escaped her chest.

He led her into his room and laid her on his couch. He sat on the edge next to her and held her hand while gently stroking the hair away from her gaunt face. Outside, he heard the birds singing sweet songs. Fragrant aromas of jasmine and oleander floated through the window from the rich garden below.

He glanced at the beautiful, breezy summer day, then down at his mother. The contrast startled him. His sweet, lovely mother was gone. This woman was unrecognizable to him. He chided himself for leaving her when she so obviously needed him and inwardly vowed never to do so again.

Over the next hour, he sat talking quietly, patting her hands, wiping her tears. Nothing he could say comforted her heart. She couldn't tell him what was wrong. Every time she started to talk, sobs, born of anger, erupted.

"We're ruined," she would say, "ruined!" And then she would sob again. "The entire town must have seen the soldiers. We'll never recover."

Whenever he asked for her to elaborate, she whimpered and cried.

"Soldiers? What soldiers?" he asked.

Her response was simply a new wave of wailing. With every breath, he prayed for wisdom and strength. When she was totally spent from her tirade, Helena finally drifted into a deep sleep. Marius quietly rose, grabbed a light blanket to cover her, and then tiptoed out of the room.

Phinneus was across the hall ordering the clean-up in Helena's room, and servants worked quietly, sweeping and mopping the chaotic mess. When Phinneus saw his master, he quickly bowed before him.

"Please have Titus meet me in the courtyard garden. Find me immediately when she awakens."

Marius nearly fled to the courtyard, avoiding all contact with all of the slaves bustling throughout the house.

Within minutes, Titus arrived, and Marius greeted him with a simple question. "What caused this?"

"My lord, it seems that early this morning, soldiers arrested Maid Livia on Governor Pliny's order."

Marius gasped, grabbing his chest as he stepped back from Titus. The color drained from his cheeks. "No," he whispered, unaware that he had voiced his shock. "Where is she now? On what charge?"

Questions tumbled out in no particular order, and Titus gently placed a hand on his forearm. Marius did not realize how close he had come to collapsing. Had Titus not steadied him, he would have disintegrated onto the ground.

"Master, I do not know many details, but I do know that Mistress Helena is angry—perhaps *furious* is a better word—at the shame that family has once again brought on your household."

Marius opened his mouth but chose not to verbalize his thoughts. After a moment, he said, "Please, give me a moment."

"Yes, my lord." Titus bowed and retreated, leaving Marius pacing throughout the garden.

He did not notice the quiet hush that had descended upon the servants. He did not notice that even the birds had left this usually peaceful spot. Nor did he notice that the breeze had died down, and the heat of the day was beating down upon him. His mind was consumed with utter sorrow. The devastation and pain he felt crashed down upon him with unbearable grief. The joy he had experienced only a couple of hours before was now replaced with intense agony. He labored to breathe, and his legs seemed unable to hold him. He crumbled down onto a marble bench, clinging to its edges while trying to absorb the shock.

He knew Livia was taken because of her Christian faith. He knew her death was imminent, and he was helpless to save her. Marius could not stop the tears. All his hopes were shattered. He shifted wearily on the cold, marble bench and closed his eyes, listening to the babble of water as it cascaded around the statue in front of him.

"No!" The word continually escaped his sobs. He had pictured the joy on her face as he shared his faith. He had thought of that moment almost non-stop for weeks. He had rehearsed how he would confess his love to her. He was still awed at the amazing change in his life because of Christ. A few years ago, he would never have allowed his mind and heart to be so consumed with a mere slave; and yet now, since his salvation, he had worshipped with believers throughout the Mediterranean, and he realized the great miracle of God's family. It was true—master and slave became family through the bond of Christ.

Marius loved this gentle woman who was so unlike any other he had ever known, and he had wanted to tell her not only of his love for her but also of his love for her Savior. And now, he would never have the chance. He cried out with no words.

Oh, Lord, I don't know what to do. Help me.

CHAPTER SIX

Cassia sat quietly against a wall, her knees drawn up to her chest with one arm wrapped around them. She bent her head toward her knees and wept. Grief painted anguished contortions on her face, and she was vaguely aware that Ezra had joined her against the wall. He covered her hand with his own and gently patted it. She was glad he was there. Sister Jaalah sat on the other side of her. She stroked Cassia's hair and waved a small fan in front of her, which Cassia found surprisingly soothing.

When Brother Justin returned, he knelt in front of her and quietly placed his massive, calloused hand on her shoulder. With a soft voice, he implored her to look at him.

"Cassia, I need to take you home. Master Marius has already left the quay. He will be home when we arrive. Perhaps he will help us." He gently helped her to her feet and pushed the hair away from her face. "Ezra, hand me that cloth."

When Ezra gave his father the cloth, Brother Justin wiped Cassia's tears with a very surprising tenderness. "Can you come with me?" he asked, grasping her hand and pulling her to her feet. He led her slowly down the steps.

When they reached the shop, Sister Jaalah straightened Cassia's tunica and tidied her hair by securing it into a quick twist at the nape of her neck. She bent down, placing a tender kiss on Cassia's forehead and hugged the child closely before turning her over to Brother Justin to begin their journey.

Ezra released his grip on her hand. Until that moment, she hadn't even noticed her dear friend was still with her. He tried to smile, but the tears in his eyes revealed the struggle in his own heart. "God go with you, my friend," he said as his voice broke.

Cassia tried to speak but could only nod. Then, she followed Brother Justin to the door.

When they were in the alley, he steadied the cart, while she obediently climbed onto the rickety seat. She held tightly to her empty basket; then in a daze, she spoke.

"I must go to the market. She'll beat me for sure if I—"

"Hush, child; don't worry about that now."

"But, sir, I mustn't return empty—"

Brother Justin seemed frustrated. "Cassia, look at me. Market can wait."

But Sister Jaalah overheard the conversation and rushed outside. She seemed to understand the child's fear and confusion. Her eyes quieted her husband, and she snatched the basket and rushed back into the shop. Within moments, she returned it to Cassia filled with many fruits and vegetables from their own table.

Cassia nodded. "Yes, yes, this will do just fine. She'll love these dates, and pomegranates are the master's favorite."

Sister Jaalah laid her hand across Cassia's. "Yes, dear. These will be fine. Now, are you ready to go?"

Cassia blinked. "I . . . I think so." Then the tears flowed again, and as Brother Justin slapped the oxen, Sister Jaalah kissed her hand and released her.

Justin urged the poor beasts to keep a dangerous pace, and except for his forceful prodding, neither he nor Cassia spoke.

When they reached Marius' estate, Justin instructed Cassia to remain with the cart while he jumped to the ground and rushed toward the main gate. However, he was stopped by her little voice. "The basket."

He shook his head and quickly retrieved her treasure, carrying it to the door and handing it to Phinneus. Phinneus looked past him to see Cassia sitting on the cart, vacantly staring at the oxen in front of her. He nodded silently to Justin and led him into the open court.

"It is not good for her to be here, my friend. I fear for her life with the mistress's present mood."

"I understand, Friend Phinneus. Perhaps I can return later. I very much wish to speak to Master Marius. When do you expect him?"

The servant glanced toward the archway and in a low whisper said, "He is here, sir, but is with his mother. I fear this is not a good time."

Justin glanced back at Cassia then toward the villa. He would not leave Cassia in a place that was not safe, but Cassia had already been gone from the villa for several hours while Justin had worked to find answers. He did not want to risk her further harm. Furthermore, he needed help to free Sisters Livia and Clio. Marius was a fair and upright man. Livia was his slave. Perhaps he could be persuaded to appeal to the proconsul on behalf of his property.

"Phinneus, I appreciate your warning, but I must speak with him. Will you please approach him and see if he will take a meeting?"

Phinneus was clearly perturbed, for he did not want to interrupt his master. Still, he could see the urgency in the carpenter's eyes. "Please wait, sir. I'll see what can be done."

When he left, he did not go to the master's chamber. Since Helena had awakened, her mood was foul, and he knew Marius had his hands full. Instead, he sought out Titus and explained the dilemma.

Titus listened and then replied, "Perhaps the master would appreciate a reprieve in his discourse. Have Justin wait in the atrium." He nodded at Phinneus and headed down the corridor.

Justin stood gazing into the rectangular pool in the center of the quad. Above him, the afternoon sun shone brightly, feeding the hungry flowers bordering this lovely space. As he slowly paced the length of the pool, he heard the raised voices above him. He stood completely still as he listened.

"I'll kill her when she returns. Do you hear me? I'll kill her. They've brought shame to this household for the last time." Helena's shrill voice overhead pierced Justin's ears.

"Mother, you mustn't speak so—"

"Do not patronize me, Marius. Those slaves have been nothing but trouble since the day we bought them. Now, the governor must surely think we are

Christians, too, since we have harbored two of their rank. I will die before I allow that brat to bring more suspicion to this home."

"Hush, Mother. I will not hear this. Governor Pliny is a gentleman of high culture and noble instincts. Furthermore, he is our friend. We have nothing to fear from him."

"Why are you fighting to keep that worthless girl?" Helena screamed. "She'll bring our destruction; I just know it. Already, I'm sure word has leaked that we have had two Christians taken by the proconsul. And both were leaders in the local movement. I'm telling you, I won't stand for it. I don't care what you do to her, but you get rid of her."

Justin heard a loud crash and instantly sucked in his breath. He had never witnessed one of Helena's famed rages. For a few minutes, all was silent, and Justin shifted from one leg to another, impatient and uncomfortable.

After many more long minutes, Phinneus arrived carrying a tray with a silver decanter. He motioned for Justin to follow. They crossed the open court through a wide walkway decorated with lush shrubs and colorful flowers. Marble statues adorned low pillars and strutted from beautifully carved benches spaced evenly along the walls. At the end of the walkway, they entered another open court, where a large fountain spewed soothing water through layers of marble basins.

The receiving room was to the left of the fountain, and Phinneus pointed to a nearby bench while he set the tray on a high shelf. "Please wait here. Master Marius will join you shortly. While you wait, can I offer you a drink?"

"No, thank you," Justin replied.

"Very well, the master will be with you soon." Phinneus bowed again before returning down the long walkway at the end of the courtyard.

A few moments later, Marius entered. His smile was broad, but his eyes were bloodshot. "Good day, Friend Justin. It is indeed a pleasure to see you." He clasped Justin's forearm and slapped him on the shoulder. "Would you like something to drink?" He retrieved the decanter and began pouring into a goblet.

Justin greeted Marius warmly but declined the hospitality. "Thank you, my lord, no. I simply came to . . ." Suddenly, Justin had no idea what he had come to say. In light of the conversation he had overheard, he shrank from approaching the subject.

Marius tilted his head, and his brows wrinkled. "Is there something wrong, my friend?"

Justin glanced at the floor, whispered a quick prayer for wisdom, then blundered ahead. He shifted his feet awkwardly as he spoke. "I came to inform you that one of your slaves—the young maid, Cassia—was at my shop delivering a message when we realized her mother was taken."

His words tumbled out of his mouth in disjointed sentences, but he forged ahead. "As she was obviously traumatized by the news, her own father so recently taken from us, my dear wife attended to her. I have just now brought her back, and I . . . " He gulped. He wished now he had accepted the wine, for his mouth was parched.

Marius did not speak but merely sipped his wine, so Justin finished his thoughts. "I wish to beg for mercy on her behalf. I know that she is late in returning from her morning errands, but her loyalty to you and your mistress is so great that she insisted we complete her tasks before returning."

Marius looked toward the peristyle, then refilled his goblet. He swept his arm toward the door, and he motioned for his guest to follow. "Would you care to take a walk with me? I should like to discuss a private matter with you."

Justin followed obediently, curious at the strange request. They went through the arched doorway and down a cobbled path toward the north gate. There, under the broad canopy of trees, Marius stopped.

"Please, sit."

Justin obeyed, and Marius seated himself on the other end of the bench.

"Do you like Ichthus?" he asked casually.

Justin paled and suddenly felt weak. He cleared his throat and closed his eyes. *Dear Lord, help me be true.* "Wh . . . what did you say, my lord?" he stalled, praying for strength.

For the first time, Marius was the one who seemed uncomfortable. He stood quickly and began pacing. "I'm sorry. I . . . I'm afraid I've been misinformed," he stuttered, and the two men waited in uncomfortable silence.

Finally, Justin spoke. His words were careful, for he recognized the terrible risk he was taking. Yet the Holy Spirit calmed him, and as he spoke, courage came. "Master Marius, I do like fish, and Ichthus is my favorite. In fact, I love it dearly. May I ask why you inquire?"

Marius returned to the bench, his eyes filled with relief. "I, too, have recently tasted Ichthus, and I have found it the most satisfying fish I have ever tasted. For years, I have sought for such satisfaction, and on this trip, I found a man who introduced me to such a . . . such a feast."

Justin's jaw dropped. *Lord, can it really be?*

"I returned, hoping to share this joy with my mother. But alas, she is not ready for it, and I . . . I am afraid I have already failed to share its . . . uh . . . its nourishment." Shame filled his eyes, and Justin could not help but think how vulnerable this mighty merchant suddenly seemed.

"Do you know, Master Marius, where the Ichthus derived its name?" Justin wanted to be sure Marius really was revealing his newfound faith.

Marius smiled. There was no fear in his eyes, for he knew he was with a brother. "Oh, yes, my friend. Iesus, CHrist, THeou, Uios, and Soter. I do indeed know its meaning; and I have met Him, and He is mine."

With a broad, infectious grin, Justin placed a hand on Marius' shoulder, and when he spoke, his voice was exuberant. "My brother, you have given me great and unexpected joy. I scarcely believe my ears. Please tell me how this came to be."

Marius smiled. "I scarcely know where to begin, my brother." He leaned in toward Justin with his hands firmly planted on his thighs and began. "For many months, Livia told me about Jesus. At first, I practically mocked her faith. But I could not deny its power in her life. She lived with such incredible peace, I wanted it. Her words haunted me, and for weeks, I sought her out nearly every day and made her tell me more. She gave me fragments of the Holy Scriptures, and I knew when she did, she was giving me her greatest treasure."

He stood then and began pacing as he continued his story. "I read the words, but I didn't really understand them. Night after night, she explained them to me, but it seemed too easy. When I left for my trip, I believed I would forget about it." He turned with a grin and stood squarely in front of Justin.

"Not only did I not forget about it, but it began to consume me." Marius began pacing again, and his hands became animated. "We had been at sea nearly three weeks traveling from port to port. I couldn't sleep. I laid awake every night wondering what was true. My whole life, I'd served the gods of Rome. I studied the stars at night and noted the vastness of the heavens. I scanned the sea throughout the day and was astonished at the immensity of its power. I knew the gods

I worshipped had to be false. Everything I saw pointed to one infinite, holy Creator; and it could not be any of the gods of Rome.

"One day, a terrible storm forced us ashore in Crete; and I stayed with a friend on the island. I know that God used that terrible storm to wash me ashore to the one man who could make it clear to me. My friend, a great nobleman on the island of Crete, had become a Christian. He had denounced the false gods of Rome and turned completely to Christ. He was brand new."

Marius plopped down next to Justin again and leaned in. "It finally all clicked—everything Livia had said, everything I had read. Everything came together, and I realized that the Bible is true. God had sent His Son, Jesus, to save me; and all I needed to do was believe on the Lord Jesus Christ to be saved."

Justin bowed his head, shaking it from side-to-side. "I did not expect this, my friend." When he looked up, Marius was gazing at him intently.

"You see, Brother," Marius continued, "I believe God sent you to me today to help me learn more of Him Who has filled my heart with peace."

"I, too, believe our Lord sent me today, and I am happy to help you grow in your faith. But alas, the reason I have come also brings sorrow to my heart."

"Ah, yes, the young maiden, Cassia—Livia's child." Marius' voice became tight, and he ended his statement at barely a whisper. He rubbed his chin and leaned forward. Sadness crept into his face, and it was so very quiet that Justin shifted uncomfortably as he sat.

Suddenly, Marius spoke, and Justin jumped slightly when he did. "I came to tell my mother of my conversion, and before I could speak, she told me about the soldiers' visit. She is angry and fears the scorn of her peers. She wants to rid our house of the scandalous Christians." He stopped and almost whispered, "I was afraid to tell her that I myself had become the thing she fears most, but now . . . " Marius shifted to face Justin again and sighed. "I don't know what to do."

His confession surprised Justin, and again, silence filled the air between them for many minutes. Justin prayed for wisdom, then eventually spoke with quiet but hopeful confidence. "You *can* do something, Master Marius. You do have options."

Marius shook his head. "Ah, my friend, there is so much you do not know. Everything I had planned for this day is destroyed. Every hope I had. Every expectation . . . " His voice trailed off; his eyes welled up with tears; and his shoulders drooped. With a slight huskiness in his voice, he continued, "You don't even realize what I hoped for today. I know this will seem shocking to you, but I actually had hopes of confessing my love to Livia." He paused. "I wanted to make her my wife."

Justin stared, dumbfounded, as Marius explained. "Livia was the one who first introduced me to Jesus. She showed me Christianity and rescued me from the sorrow and sadness that consumed me after I lost my wife and child. Somewhere along the way, I discovered that I loved her. And now, she'll never know." He stood and sighed, kicking at a pebble on the path.

"Does Sister Livia have any clue that you feel so strongly for her?" Justin asked, not entirely surprised. He remembered several times when Sister Livia had rejoiced with their church body because of her opportunities to point Marius to Christ. Justin also remembered Jaalah warning Livia only a few months before when Livia was sharing the depth of her conversations with Marius. Jaalah had sensed that Livia was developing stronger feelings for her master and had cautioned her to guard her heart.

Marius only shook his head and replied, "No, she doesn't. She has no idea."

Justin stood and placed his hand on Marius's shoulder. "Marius, my brother, I do not know what God has planned for you; but I can tell you that without His intervention, she will never have an opportunity to hear of the changes in your heart. What I do know is that there is a little girl out there whose heart is breaking and who needs our help. I believe you can help not only Sisters Livia and Cassia, but also another sister in Christ named Clio."

He cleared his throat. "They are in terrible peril. I am trying to gain a meeting with the proconsul to beg for mercy on their behalf, but I am merely a carpenter. Perhaps . . . perhaps you would consider speaking to him yourself. You are a well-respected merchant who, I am told, dines frequently with the esteemed governor."

"I . . . " Marius hesitated. "I would like to help, my friend, but . . . . The truth is, I am afraid." He dropped his gaze and closed his eyes, shaking his head from side to side.

Justin's voice was quiet at first, but soon, his passionate prayer reverberated through the garden. "Lord, thank You for the work you have done in

Master Marius's life. Thank You for drawing him to You. We come to You now, for only You can help us. We are afraid. We need guidance. We need courage, and, Lord, we ask for a miracle for Sisters Livia and Clio. Help us do what we ought to do. And, Lord, we've seen You work a miracle in Master Marius, and we ask the same with Mistress Helena. Help her see You are the only One Who can give her peace. Finally, Lord, please comfort Cassia. Protect her and give her hope." Brother Justin continued to pray, his voice lifted to Heaven.

Suddenly, Marius grasped his burly arm, interrupting the older man's prayer. "My friend, I know what to do."

Justin smiled, ignoring the unconventional interruption. He listened expectantly as Marius spoke.

"Gather your assembly together for prayer. I seem to remember a passage from the Holy Scriptures where a Jewish queen was brought to her kingdom for such a time as to save her people from destruction. I will pray, as she did, and ask the Lord to direct our actions. I will do my part to save these women."

Justin did not realize that he had been holding his breath. But as soon as Marius finished speaking, Justin released a heavy sigh and nearly shouted,

"Thank you, my lord. I will spread the word immediately, and may God go with you." Justin turned to go, but then stopped. "And what about the young maiden?"

Marius smiled with obvious hope and began walking back toward the main atrium. Justin followed, nearly jogging to keep up.

"You asked for mercy for the slave. I grant it to you. The slave girl shall be free. I will draw up the manumission papers at once, and I place her in your hands until we can resolve everything else. I pray God goes with you both. She has sacrificed much for the cause of Christ. We have much work to do for Livia and—I'm sorry, what is the other woman's name?"

"Clio"

"Yes, Clio. I need to arrange some things here, and then I'll meet you at your shop as quickly as I can so we can plan our next step."

When they finally reached the front gate, Marius chuckled. "Mother believes Cassia's dismissal will rid us once and for all of the shame of Christianity, but she is merely trading one Christian slave child for a Christian son instead. Please pray for me to have wisdom to share His love with steadfast courage."

"Thank you, my brother," Justin exclaimed, his voice tight with emotion.

"Think not of it again, my brother. God granted this woeful sinner a merciful pardon. I can think of no better way to show my gratitude to Him than to offer hope to another sister in need."

"Sisters," Justin reminded him with a grin, and Marius laughed.

Justin exited the estate and climbed onto the cart. He slapped the reins and jolted with the cart as the oxen began to lumber toward town. "Oh, Cassia, you won't believe what just happened." The startled child looked at him with her swollen, red eyes. "Cassia, the master has set you free. You are coming to live with us. Do you understand that? He set you free." Justin pulled on the reins, and the oxen stopped.

"Cassia, you are free." Tears formed in his eyes. "I begged God for mercy, child, but my faith was weak. You have no idea what God has done." He put his big, burly arm around her shoulders and let out a shout. "Hallelujah. Hallelujah!"

"And what about my mother?" Her voice hiccupped as the tears rimmed her eyes again.

He sat still, looking into her scared, dark eyes. "Mercy. We'll keep praying for mercy and see what

God decides." She rested her head against his chest, and he slapped the reins again.

CHAPTER SEVEN

A soldier yanked Livia by the ropes that joined her wrists tightly together. He led her from the basilica after her trial and forced her into an open courtyard that was covered with sand and hay. She noted several spots of blood tainting the earth, and she was afraid.

She stumbled trying to keep up with the soldier's insane pace. When she did, he yanked her wrists even harder, almost lifting her off of the ground and practically dragging her to the center of the arena. When they finally stopped, she looked up and realized they stood in front of several tall, wide, wooden posts jutting like monstrous claws out of the ground.

He slammed her into one of the posts, and her face bounced off the unyielding wood. She heard a crunching sound; and immediately, pain, like white-hot branding irons searing her nose, consumed her. A gush of liquid oozed into her mouth and she coughed, sputtering blood and mucous onto her forearms. She could sense the displacement of her nose and tried to lift her bound hands to her face. She fought to catch her breath while choking on the excess blood. Dazed and confused, every movement seemed slow and disconnected.

Livia sobbed out loud as the soldier pulled out a large knife and cut the ropes tying her wrists together. Then he sneered; and an ugly, vile smile turned up the corners of his lips. He ripped her tunica down to her waist and slapped her arms away when she tried to cover herself.

"Grab those two rings," he ordered, pointing to two metal circles dangling just above her head on either side of the wooden post. She grabbed the ring on the right side obediently but noticed that she couldn't see the ring on the left side. She touched her face near her eye. The flesh on her eyebrow was torn, and her eyelid was swollen. She wanted to inspect the wound more, but the soldier yanked her hand and placed it on the ring.

With her body facing the beam, he tied her hands to each ring. He pulled the ropes so tight that she cried out in agony. He just laughed.

While she stood in humiliation, another soldier brought Clio and repeated the same cruel indecency.

"Clio! Are you all right?" Livia asked her friend.

"I'm—" Clio's words were cut off by a smack on the back of her head.

"Silence!" Clio's soldier screamed.

The soldiers stepped off to the side, and before Livia could follow them with her eyes, the first sting of the whip scourged her back. She shrieked while her entire body convulsed in response.

After the flogging, she struggled to remain conscious. She was vaguely aware of being dragged out of the arena, and somehow, she ended up in what seemed like a darkened cave. Hearing Clio weeping behind her, she cried out, "'He will never leave [us], nor forsake [us]'"[4] as they descended step by cold, stone step into darkness.

The guards tossed the women against a wall and then clamped heavy chains to their wrists. The pain was all-consuming. She cried with every movement. When the guards left the chamber, Livia begged them to leave a torch. She heard their cruel laughter as they secured the massive iron gate and walked away. As the darkness encompassed her, she quickly faded into unconsciousness.

Livia lay on the uneven ground of the prison and tried to maneuver her arms so she could check the shooting pain in her forearm. The iron clamps

---

4 Hebrews 13:5

at each wrist and the short chains connecting her to the wall made all movement cumbersome. But the pain was intensifying.

She shifted just enough to feel a welt, and it throbbed under her fingertips. She could feel torn flesh. She didn't remember the whip slicing into her arm at all. She shuddered, shaking her head violently, trying to erase the flashes of all that had happened. From the moment she had arrived at the basilica to her trial with the proconsul, Livia's brain quickly rehashed the myriad events she had experienced. But then images of the most terrible moments rushed into her mind, and she relived each horrible second.

Shaking her head in the darkness now, Livia rebelled. "No. No!" she sobbed, refusing to let herself relive every agonizing moment. She rubbed her forearm again, feeling the deep cut and realizing that the leather strips on the whip must have missed the intended target of her back and ripped into her forearm. Now, in utter darkness, she could neither inspect the wound nor fully relieve the pain. The darkness, which only hours before had sent shudders of terror through her slender, broken frame, now covered her, almost peacefully, by concealing the grotesque wounds that were swelling and oozing from nearly every inch of her arm, back, and legs.

Sprawled face-down on the damp, rocky, clay floor of the prison, she fought to remain conscious. The coolness of the earth revived her. And with her cheek resting against the firmness of the floor, the spinning sensation in her head seemed more secure. In the intense darkness, she could not determine if the whipping had caused her vision loss or if the blackness just erased it. She could sense the swelling above her left eye was more pronounced but found strange comfort in closing both eyes and embracing the muddy terrain beneath her.

Another wave of nausea overtook her, and without grace or dignity, she wretched, tasting the bitter acid as it bubbled and foamed past her bruised lips. During the second heave, the acrid liquid spewed from her nostrils and seared her swollen nose. She cried out again as she pushed herself away from the foul remnants of her gut and tried to roll onto her side.

She heard a deep moan. It seemed muddled and distant, yet she knew somehow that it was her own groaning. "Lord, take me quickly," she prayed as she pressed her face into the cool clay just a few inches from her vomit.

She again wrapped her fingers around the searingly hot skin on her forearm and tried to rub away the pain. Every sensation was disorienting and hazy. She seemed to be gasping for air and breathing deeply at the same time; and in her confusion, she gulped in some mud. She cried out as she sputtered and choked on the mouthful of dirt and shifted her lips away from the ground.

She heard moaning again; but this time, it came from farther away. She tried to push herself up but struggled with the chains shackled around her wrists. She used what little strength she had to force herself into a sitting position and then scooted closer to the stone wall of the cave in order to relieve the strain of the chains on her limbs. Every movement shot pain through her back. The clanking noise of the heavy iron links confused her senses.

She pushed against the hard earth trying to get more comfortable, and the pain shot through her forearm again. She couldn't be sure, but it felt like blood was dripping from the wound down to her fingertips, and the sensation frightened her.

"Livia." She heard her name but could not respond. The voice was raspy, barely above a whisper, yet Livia distinctly recognized her name. She sat completely still and heard nothing but the plink, plink, plink of water incessantly dripping one annoying droplet at a time from some cracked joint in the boulders above her. And then, she heard it again.

"Livia." This time, the voice sounded familiar. Livia shook her head again, trying to concentrate. "It's me, Livia. It's Clio."

Overcome with gratitude, Livia sobbed. "Clio! Oh, Clio. You're here," she moaned. The tears didn't come one at a time, nor were they stifled by her normal sense of propriety. No, these tears erupted from a place of anguish so deep that they burst from the depth of her soul into the terrorizing darkness, and they burned when they passed over the swollen rims of her eyes. She wailed. Deep, agonizing cries escaped with each breath. She couldn't breathe, and her labored gasps for air were the only things interrupting the sadness as it poured out of her.

Clio cried, too. Livia heard the same pain pouring forth from her friend. Neither could console the other. Many minutes passed. Or maybe it was hours. Livia had no sense of time. But eventually, there was nothing left to release. The sorrow wasn't gone, but the tears did subside for both of them. And when they did, the women comforted one another by communing in the darkness.

"How long do you think we'll be here?" Clio asked.

"Not long," Livia replied. "We've already had our trial; and since neither of us recanted, even after our punishment, it will only be a few days at the most."

"How long have we been here already?" Clio's voice quivered.

"I don't know. I honestly have no idea." Livia shivered. "I can barely piece together what's happened. I'm not fully aware of things. I don't think I've been quite conscious." She gingerly leaned against the cold, stone wall of the cave, flinching until she found a more comfortable position.

"I feel the same way," Clio replied. "Do you think this is what the apostle Paul meant when he wasn't sure if he was in the body or out of the body?"

Livia almost smiled. "That's how I feel. I can't figure out if I'm really awake or not."

She tried to go back to the beginning. She replayed the moment she saw the soldiers at the villa. After her triggering encounter with the ring-necked dove, Livia had rushed to her room and sought refuge from her ominous thoughts. From her perch under the eaves of the villa, she had clearly heard the horses when they came, and she had glanced out the small window above the low bench in the corner of her tiny room. She knew they were coming for her, so she had knelt by her bed and prayed.

And they did come. Just like they had come for her husband two years before. She was summoned to the courtyard, and the captain had unrolled a scroll before her and read the proclamation placing her under arrest. He had ordered her hands bound and marched her out of the courtyard and through the iron gates of the villa. Once she had reached the road, she saw Sister Clio.

"Was it just this morning when they took us?" Livia asked. She wanted to rub the pounding pain at her temples, but the shackles made every movement of her arms cumbersome. The chains clanked so loudly that she did not hear Clio's reply, but it didn't matter. She was spent. She groaned as she leaned her head against the cave wall. Every part of her hurt.

With her eyes closed, she pictured her last glimpse of Cassia. "Oh, Lord, protect my darling girl," she prayed. Fresh tears escaped through her closed eyes, and she hiccupped the sobs that forced their way up from her chest. She pictured Justin carrying Cassia to safety, and she found great comfort in that vision.

Clio's whimper interrupted her reverie, and Livia comforted her. "It won't be long, my friend, until all our pain is gone. Soon, we'll be walking with our Savior face-to-face. We're almost home now."

"Yes, we're almost home." Clio's voice was barely a whisper.

Livia leaned her head against the stone and fought hard to remain conscious. She heard Clio rehearsing their descent into the prison and relived the same panic.

"Thank you, my sister, my friend," whispered Clio. "Thank you for helping me finish my race strong. I can say with the great apostle, 'I have kept the faith.'"[5]

She roused to reply, "Oh, Clio, how grateful I am to be entering glory with you. He is here with us. He has given us the comfort of each other during this dark hour. Oh, Lord, take us quickly."

Her last thoughts before she drifted into another haze was of Master Marius. She pictured him standing before her. She envisioned his handsome face and smiled when she thought of the way he always ran his hand through his hair when she made him think too hard about something. "Save him, dear Father. Please help him find You."

Despite her pain, Livia drifted in and out of a dazed slumber. How long she battled consciousness she did not know, but eventually, she heard her name again.

"Livia. Livia, are you still here? Are you still with me?" Clio's voice was frantic. "Livia, please, please wake up! Please don't leave me yet! They're coming for us. Please, Livia. They're coming."

---

5 2 Timothy 4:7

Livia roused enough to groan. Clio cried out in relief. "Oh, Livia. This is it. They're coming. They're coming for us."

Livia turned her head toward Clio's voice. "Clio?"

"Oh, Livia, I'm so afraid. I can hear them coming, and I see the light."

Livia tried to open her eyes. They seemed heavy and unresponsive, but she fought hard to open them. The darkness of the cave was still overwhelming, but she noticed the change, too. She squinted. "I think I can see you, Clio," she whispered, noting the faint, misty glow behind the dark outline of a form.

"How will they do it?" Clio asked. "How will they execute us? I'm so afraid, Livia."

"Hush, Clio. It'll be over soon. Our Father is with us." Livia watched the light become brighter as the torchbearers descended into the cave. Soon, she heard voices, and she waited. "I'm ready, Father." She closed her eyes and sank into an almost blissful stupor.

CHAPTER EIGHT

Marius sat in the carriage barking orders to Titus. Phinneus sat across them taking inventory of the baskets of supplies next to him—linen strips, oils, skins of water, bread, fruit, ointments, shawls, pillows, an oil lamp, and opiates. "Titus, when we get to the palace grab the supplies. Phinneus, take the carriage and head into town and replace any supplies we'll need until this ordeal is done. I don't care if we have hours or days; I don't want Livia to suffer any more than she has to."

"Yes, my lord," both men responded.

"And, Phinneus, make sure you get those items for Cassia as well."

"Yes, my lord," the old servant replied.

Marius opened the scroll in his hands and read it again. The jostling of the carriage thwarted his efforts, but he knew what the letter said. He wiped sweat from his brow, and Titus reached to pull back the curtain to let in some fresh air. Marius waved him back. "No need, Titus; we're almost there."

The carriage turned into the palace grounds, and Marius' breaths came in shorter bursts. He suddenly felt like he couldn't fill up his lungs. He folded the scroll again and stared ahead, waiting for the carriage to stop. When it did, he jumped out, not waiting for Phinneus to prepare the way as he normally would. Justin was just ahead of him helping a woman from a cart. Marius bounded toward them and held the scroll. "I have our permission," he stated.

"Good, then we should not have any trouble." Justin replied, but he put a hand on Marius' arm. "Just remember, my friend, we don't know what we'll find."

"Yes. Yes, I remember." Marius nodded. "But I can handle it." He turned to enter the prison gate when he heard a gentle rebuke from Justin.

"And this is my dear wife, Jaalah."

Marius whipped around with his mouth agape. "My dear woman, please forgive me." He bowed low and humbly extended his hand toward her. At first, he didn't notice the mirth in either Justin's or Jaalah's eyes; but once he heard her reply, he snapped his head to see their amusement.

"Clearly, mine is not the face you are seeking," Jaalah calmly stated. Justin threw his head back with a hearty laugh while Jaalah merely smiled at Marius.

"I—"

"Think nothing of it, Master Marius," Jaalah interrupted. "But since I'm really *not* the person you so desperately want to see, let's just save more intimate introductions until later." She winked and reached her arm through Justin's as they turned toward the prison entrance.

Marius practically ran to the gate while Justin, Jaalah, and Titus followed behind laden with all of the supplies. Marius commanded the soldier to give them entrance, and he tapped his foot impatiently while the guard read the document.

The guard pounded his staff against the ground, and another soldier came forth. "Take them to the prisoners," the guard ordered, handing the scroll to the soldier. The soldier glanced at the scroll and responded to the guard by thumping his clenched right fist over his heart and bowing slightly. He turned immediately away from Marius without a word. Marius quickly followed and never once looked back at his entourage.

They followed a long, covered pathway to an open quadrangle. Other soldiers stood watch over various entryways that spilled into the courtyard from each corner. The soldier led them to a long wall near the end. They turned north, and the path narrowed between the stone wall on their left and a two-story stone building on their right. Marius assumed the building was the soldiers' barracks but barely took notice of it. At the end of the narrow path stood the arched entrance to the prison.

The soldier grabbed two torches and handed one to Marius. Again, without a word, they began their descent into the darkness. Marius glanced over his shoulder, and a nod from Justin assured him that they were all still with him. Marius tried to hold the torch toward them so they could navigate the crumbling stone steps more carefully. As they wound their way down the spiral stone staircase, all light from the setting sun disappeared. The darkness grew eerily thick.

Marius heard Jaalah yelp and immediately turned the torch more fully toward them. He saw Justin shift their basket to one hand while steadying his wife with the other, and Marius's face heated in shame. He reached for the basket, and Justin gladly released it to him. Marius briefly thought about how much of his aristocratic, authoritarian manners he needed to change; but he also knew this was not the time for self-reflection. Livia was at the bottom of this pit, and that was all that mattered to him.

When they were nearing the last bend of their descent, a filthy stench overwhelmed him. Marius gagged and nearly vomited. Jaalah, too, seemed to be struggling, but the soldier didn't wait for them to recover. Marius raised the torch toward Jaalah, and she sputtered, "Just keep going; we're almost there."

It pained Marius to know that Justin and Jaalah had been through this process before. How many others had there been? How many of their friends had they tended to in this despicable place? He refused to ask the last question that popped into his mind. He knew the answer—*none*. None had been saved. None of their friends had ever left this prison alive.

For a moment, he thought he might collapse; but he steadied himself with an arm against the wall, gathered his senses, and willed himself to continue. The humidity made it hard to breathe, and the horrific blend of odors almost overwhelmed him. Human feces, mixed with mold and other vile smells, permeated the air. To him, it smelled like death.

At last, they reached the final step and gathered in the small landing. Before them was the entrance to the cave. Two massive, wooden beams were wedged between the low rock above their heads and the graveled bedrock at their feet. An iron gate was hung on the beams, and the soldier placed his torch in a rusty sconce on the wall. He pulled out a large, metal key that dangled from his belt; and in the near darkness, he clumsily fiddled to open the lock.

Marius deftly tilted his own torch toward the soldier's hands, and finally, he heard the clunk of the lock release the gate. The soldier stood aside to let them enter, and Marius rushed past him.

"Put the torch on the ground when we get in," Justin said. "It'll give off more light," he explained. Marius nodded and then ducked beneath the low ceiling of the cave.

Once inside, he held the torch for the others, and when they were all inside, he slowly panned it around the room. At first, all he saw was the jagged edges of rock; but a soft whimper near the entrance made him lower the torch. There on the floor near his feet was Clio. Jaalah immediately rushed to her side.

Marius scanned the lower edges of the wall, and when he saw Livia, he cried out.

Justin touched his arm. "Put the torch on the ground, my friend."

Marius obeyed and crouched low, moving slowly toward her.

"Livia?" He knew the disfigured body in front of him was Livia, but he was shattered by her appearance.

The torchlight flashed chillingly in the darkness, and Marius just stood with his mouth ajar. Justin and Titus each fumbled to light the oil lamps; and once they did, they all got a better look at the women before them.

"Livia?" Marius said her name again, but she didn't move.

He dropped to his knees, tears stinging his eyes, and he grabbed her hand. When he did, she let out a low moan, and he openly wept. "Oh, Livia," he cried. "You're still with me." He turned to Titus. "She's still alive!"

Titus was kneeling on the other side of Livia. After soaking several linen cloths, he handed the waterskin to Marius. "She'll need to drink."

Marius grabbed the water and gently lifted it to Livia's mouth. She sputtered and coughed when he first offered it, but he slowed down and just barely dribbled it onto her mouth. She never opened her eyes but began to swallow the liquid as it passed through her lips. He rejoiced that she was alive.

Titus handed him a cloth, and he tried to wipe the blood from her face. She winced the moment the cool rag touched her cheek. "Oh, Livia, don't be afraid. I'm here. I won't hurt you." He stroked her forehead and dabbed the cloth on her face again. This time, her eyes fluttered. He could see she was fighting to open them, and he ran his finger across her eyebrow almost willing her to look at him.

"Livia, I'm here," he soothed. "I'm here."

If he hadn't been looking at her, he would not have heard her whimper his name, but she did. With obvious effort, she moved her lips and simply said, "Master."

"Yes, Livia. Yes. It's me. I'm here." She forced her eyelids open and squinted against the light. At first, her eyes rolled wildly, so Marius leaned in close. "I'm here, Livia. I'm right beside you."

She closed her eyes in a long, slow blink. When she opened them again, he could tell that she recognized him. "Oh, Master," she sobbed. "Master."

Chapter Nine

"Master?" Livia whispered his name again. Her eyes fluttered as she fought to escape the heavy fog in her brain. His face seemed only inches from her own, but she convinced herself she was dreaming. She refused to move her eyes from his.

"Livia, I am here."

She heard his voice but still distrusted her senses. His hands gently stroked her forehead, and she tried to reach her own hand to touch his face. The iron clamps at her wrists assured her that she wasn't dreaming, but she still struggled to comprehend the hallucination that made her believe Marius was with her.

"Master," she whimpered again. Only this time, she added, "Marius," with the faintest sigh.

"Oh, Livia, I'm here. I'm really here. Look at me. Here." He lifted her hand to his face. "Touch me. I'm real."

He held her palm against his cheek, and she slowly ran her thumb along the firm edge of his jaw. He leaned his cheek into her hand, and she felt his breath as he whispered against her. "Oh, Livia, my precious Livia."

She roused, rather startled at his words, and tried to lean forward to see him more clearly. It was true. He was real. And he was with her. Her tears flowed unhindered, and she stared openly into his eyes. *Precious.* Had she really heard that word? No. He wouldn't have called her precious, but he was here. He was holding her hand and talking softly to her, and that was enough.

"Here, drink some more," he gently commanded, and he held the waterskin to her lips. As he tilted it toward her, some water dribbled down her chin; but once its coolness entered her mouth, she turned her attention to it. She suddenly felt greedy for the soothing liquid and gulped it down.

Marius pulled it away. "Drink slowly, Livia. Give your body time to take it in." He put the skin back to her lips, and she tried to obey. However, she desperately craved more. After several large swallows, Marius pulled it back again. "We'll give you more in a moment."

The water revived her. She felt it flow down her throat, past her chest, and into her stomach. Once it did, she thought she might vomit again; and she focused all of her energy on settling the nausea.

Marius wiped her forehead again with the cloth, and its coolness calmed her.

"Livia, this is going to sting a little bit, but it won't last long." She couldn't make out the voice, but she was aware that someone else was tending to the wound on her arm. She felt him pour water over it, and then she cried out when he poured some kind of ointment over it.

Marius leaned in closely. "Look at me, Livia." She obeyed but whimpered in pain. "Titus is cleaning your wounds. It might hurt, but it won't last long. You'll feel better soon."

Livia locked her eyes with Marius's and tried not to cry out as Titus began wrapping her wound. Marius kept wiping her forehead and cheeks with the cloth, and he talked tenderly to her whenever she grimaced in pain.

Eventually, Titus moved closer to her face. "Livia, can you lean forward? I need to check your back."

She tried to move but had no strength.

"Let me help you." Marius did not wait for her reply but gently placed both of his arms under her armpits and lifted her forward. She cried out when he moved her and nearly fainted. She heard him gasp, and when he spoke, his voice was tight with emotion.

"Oh, Livia, I'm so sorry. I'm. . ." His voice cracked, and he finished with a whisper in her ear. "I'm so very sorry, my precious one."

She heard it again. He had called her his precious one. She couldn't understand why, but it sounded beautiful to her.

She flinched in pain as Titus worked on her back and was forced to focus on enduring the pain while he cleaned each wound and poured ointment into them. When he was finally done, Marius lowered her back against the wall.

Titus prepared a cup of medicine and lifted it to her lips. "Drink this, Livia. It's bitter; but it will help with the pain, and it will help you rest."

She tried to obey; but the medicine was so bitter, she turned away.

Marius took the cup from Titus. "Look at me, Livia." He leaned his face close to hers again, and she locked her eyes on his. "I know this is horrible, but it will help you. Can you drink it for me?"

She nodded and somehow managed to swallow each bitter gulp that he poured into her mouth. Next, he held a date to her mouth and said, "Eat." He fed her several dates bite by bite and then gave her more water to drink.

By the time she had finished drinking the last bit of liquid in the waterskin, she felt stronger and more revived. While Marius fed her, Titus had covered her with a blanket and had even positioned a soft pillow behind her back. She couldn't tell if the food and water made her feel so much better or if Titus's horrible medicine did; but by the time Marius set the waterskin back in the basket, she felt immense relief.

"I'm leaving some food here in this basket, Livia." Titus moved the basket right next to her good arm while he continued giving her instructions. "There's enough oil in the lamp to give you light for at least two hours. But you have more oil and more wicks in the basket. You've also got flint right here." He took her hand and placed it on the side of the basket so she could feel the flint. "Do you understand?"

When she nodded, he continued. "You have two more waterskins as well. Try to drink as much as you can but go slowly."

"Thank you, friend Titus," she managed to say. "Thank you so much."

"I'm sorry this plight has befallen you, Livia," Titus replied. "But we'll try to make you as comfortable as possible."

Livia turned back to look at Marius. "Thank you, Master."

He reached and stroked her cheek again. "Oh, Livia, I'm so sorry. I'm so very sorry for you."

They heard the guard yell, "Time's up" outside the gate and heard the clanking of the chains as he fiddled to unlock the door.

Marius swallowed hard, leaned in close, and whispered against her ear, "Oh, Livia, I don't know if I'll see you again, but I must tell you this. I have come to know your Savior. He is mine, Livia. I believe in the Lord Jesus Christ."

He pulled away from her, and she grabbed at his chest. "Is this true, Master? Can it really be?"

"It is, Livia! It is true!"

Livia's joy permeated her battered face, and she smiled. "Oh, Master! You cannot possibly know my joy."

She wanted to ask a thousand questions so badly, but the guard's voice bellowed, "Time's up. You must leave immediately."

Marius started to stand and said, "I don't know if we can come back, but I promise you we'll try."

Livia grasped his hand, and he knelt close to her a moment longer. "Master, please . . . please take care of Cassia."

"Oh, Livia, I promise to take care of her. I'm granting her manumission. She will live as a free Roman citizen the rest of her days."

Livia's eyes widened, and with the faintest cry, she whispered, "Oh, thank you, Master. Thank you." As the tears spilled down her face, she watched him leave. *Thank you, God, for saving him and for leading him to set Cassia free.* She knew that she could die in peace.

When the guard locked the gate, she saw Marius lift his hand in a tentative wave, and then he was gone. She closed her eyes, and sweet slumber quickly overtook her weary body.

CHAPTER TEN

Marius stood next to Justin's cart outside the prison. Sister Jaalah sat in the cart and cried while the men talked. Tears flowed freely from both men as they discussed their options.

"How can they survive this? I've never seen such suffering." Marius wept as he spoke.

Justin leaned in and quietly asked, "Did you tell her of your conversion?"

Marius looked over his shoulder to see that Titus was busy loading supplies into his carriage and then turned back to Brother Justin. "I did." He wiped his cheek as he leaned in and continued, "She was so happy. I don't know how she could have such joy while enduring such pain, but I hope it encourages her to know that her efforts on my behalf were not in vain."

"Hopefully, we can get permission to see them again tomorrow. Until then, we have much to do. Have faith." Justin climbed into the cart. "We'll keep praying for a miracle," he said as he slapped the reins on the oxen. "We still have hope."

Marius wiped away more tears and returned to his carriage. "Follow the carpenter," he barked to his driver, but he did not speak to either Titus or Phinneus. Instead, he used the silence to think through all of the tasks ahead of him. He had filed an appeal on behalf of Livia and Clio and planned to follow up with the magistrate in the morning. He had also secured an official meeting with the governor. When he had asked for the meeting, Pliny had invited Marius and Helena to dine with him and his wife Calpurnia. The meeting was to be the following evening after the meal.

Marius also needed to complete the manumission papers for Cassia and Livia. He knew Livia was about to die, but he wanted her to die free. He also wanted her to die knowing that he would provide for Cassia's every need. He glanced at the basket next to Phinneus in the carriage. He could see that Phinneus had been successful in purchasing new clothing and supplies for Cassia, and he smiled in gratitude that he had such trustworthy servants. His plan was to drop off Cassia's new garments at Justin's home and then to get to his estate as quickly as possible.

However, when he arrived at Justin's, Cassia bounded down the stairs and asked if her mother was free yet. Her breathless expectation stabbed at his soul. Kneeling beside her, he looked her straight in the eye, held her hand, and promised, "I'm trying my best." It broke him to see her high hopes when he knew there was so little chance of gaining Livia's freedom.

"Sweet Cassia, can you look at me?" He lifted her chin with his finger and gazed into her dark brown eyes as tears formed in his.

Suddenly, she pushed away from his chest and glared at him. "Is Mother . . . g-gone?" she asked bravely, bracing against the news.

"Oh, no, no, my child. Please forgive me. Your mother is weak, but we gave her food and medicine. I could tell it made her feel better, and when we left, she was resting."

Tears flowed down Cassia's still-bruised cheeks. "Oh, Mother," she whispered, all the sorrow of her young, broken heart uttered in those two words.

Marius reached his arm around her thin shoulders and clumsily offered comfort. He dared not tell her how frail and broken Livia and Clio had appeared. Instead, he simply nodded. "Her spirit is strong. She is weak, but she assured me that our God is faithful. She misses you very much, and she wants you to know how happy she is that you are safe. I promised her I would take care of you."

"Oh, Mother." Cassia buried her head into her hands and wept.

On impulse, he gathered her in his arms, choking back emotion.

She easily surrendered to his embrace, and when he released her, she reached a hand to wipe away the single tear that escaped down his cheek. "Don't cry, Master. It's going to be okay." Her simple faith rebuked him.

Jaalah entered with a tray of fruit, and Justin followed with a decanter. Marius politely declined. He directed his conversation to Cassia but made sure Justin and Jaalah understood his intent. "I've brought some clothing and supplies for you, Cassia. If you need anything at all, you must let me know because I promised your mother I would take care of you."

He glanced up at his hosts and emphasized, "I mean that."

They all watched with delight as Cassia pulled out the pretty tunicas from the basket. "Are these really for me?" she squealed, and they all laughed.

When Cassia had examined each beautiful item, Jaalah offered to help her put them away in her room. The child hugged Marius and thanked him with a kiss on the cheek. Marius choked back his emotion and watched them climb the stairs to their home.

He and Justin briefly discussed their plans for the following day, and then Marius departed. When he arrived at his estate, Marius rushed to his room, closed the door, knelt down by his bed, and wept. Through tears and pain, he poured out his soul to God and begged for mercy on Livia's behalf. Her bruised, swollen face and shredded back filled his thoughts, and he could not shake the images from his mind.

He also thought of Cassia and admitted to himself that he wanted to keep her and raise her as his own child. She was Livia's child, and she had become more precious to him each day since Livia had been taken.

Whenever he would arrive at Justin's home, she would exclaim her delight and usually vault into his lap and burrow her head against his chest. He could not help but smile. It was something he was not used to, but when he had promised her he would try to save Livia, she had begun to shower her affection on him whenever he visited. He loved every moment of it and was reminded of how much he missed his own sweet Julia. Cassia was not replacing Julia in his mind, but she was reminding him of how much he loved being a father.

Marius climbed onto his bed and covered his face with his hands. "Please, God, please save Livia."

CHAPTER ELEVEN

Marius left his villa before dawn. He reached the basilica before the first rays of sun crept through the morning sky. Soldiers guarded the entrance to the magistrates' offices, and he knew he would have to wait an hour or two to gain entrance. He only cared about seeing Livia again, and waiting to be first in line with the magistrate was an easy sacrifice to accomplish that goal.

Titus sat across from him in the carriage and fought hard to stifle a yawn. Marius also yawned, and the stress of the last few days showed on his weary face. He rubbed his forehead and closed his eyes.

He jolted upright when he heard the soldiers talking outside, and he realized he had dozed off. He opened the carriage door and told Titus to stay with the supplies. He then paced around the grounds in front of the entrance of the basilica, glancing at the doors every few minutes.

He noticed a handful of townspeople entering the thoroughfare, and he bounded up the steps and stood in front of the soldiers to wait. Within moments, the heavy, wooden doors were opened from within; and the soldiers stepped aside to let him enter.

He practically ran to the back of the hallway and submitted his name to the soldier outside the magistrate's office. When he was called into the office, the plump, balding magistrate simply handed him a scroll. "That will get you back into the prison again," he muttered, "and I've referred your appeal to the governor. It is out of my hands now."

He never raised his eyes to look at Marius and merely shooed him away with the wave of his hand. Marius never bothered to thank him but grasped the scroll and bowed before exiting the room.

Once back in the great hallway, he followed it toward the wide staircase in the center of the room. A din of people gathered around various doorways near each office door, and Marius hoped his next stop would not have a long line. He took the stairs two at a time and reached the landing in seconds. To his relief, no one stood outside the door of the manumission magistrate. He gave his name to the guard and only had to wait a few minutes before he was called.

Once inside, the magistrate smiled and wished him good day. Marius bowed and approached the pleasant-looking man, not much older than himself, who sat behind the large table. The magistrate rose and shook Marius's hand and motioned for him to sit.

Marius sat on the bench opposite the magistrate. He wiped at the beads of sweat that had formed across his forehead and waited.

The magistrate turned toward a large bookshelf on the wall next to him and rifled through several scrolls that were placed between the narrow, vertical slats of the shelves. After examining three scrolls and returning them to their place on the shelf, he finally pulled out the ones he was seeking. "Ah, yes, here they are." He turned back toward Marius and unfolded each scroll. "If everything meets your approval, you only need to sign at the bottom of each page."

Marius examined the documents, then reached for the metal stylus. He dipped the tip into the ink, scrawled his signature, and handed the papers back. The magistrate held a small stick of wax over a flame until small droplets of wax formed. He held each scroll under the wax and then imprinted his seal.

When the wax on each scroll was cooled, he handed them back to Marius. "That completes the process, Master Marius. Your slaves are officially free."

Marius bowed and thanked the magistrate. He placed the scrolls in the leather satchel that hung across his body and trotted outside and back to his carriage.

"Head to the prison," he ordered his driver as he entered the carriage. Once inside, he turned to Titus. "We have our permission to see them again."

The carriage rounded the basilica and arrived at the prison quadrangle behind the ornate government buildings. Before the wheels had completely stopped turning, Marius opened the carriage door and jumped down. Brother Justin and Sister Jaalah were once again waiting for him, and he jogged over to their cart.

He grabbed the basket from their cart while Justin helped Jaalah descend. "Good morning, my friends," he said, bowing toward them. "Everything is in order." He held out the scroll from the magistrate.

They repeated their journey into the prison, and Marius experienced the same nausea at the bottom of the stairs. It was all he could do not to vomit. When they reached the cell this time, they noticed a soft glow coming from inside.

Marius heaved a sigh of relief knowing that the women had not run out of oil during the night. "At least, they haven't had to live in utter darkness," he said as they waited for the guard to unlock the bolt.

When they were inside the cell, he rushed to Livia's side. She was awake, and she smiled as soon as she saw him. "You came back." She sighed.

"Yes, Livia, I came back. And I'll come back every single day until . . . "

"Until I'm in glory," she finished for him. "It's okay, Master. I'm going home. Don't be sad."

"Oh, Livia, there's so much I hoped for, so much I wanted to tell you."

She winced as Titus began tending to the wound on her arm. Marius checked the wound as Titus poured water over it. He looked back at Livia. "It looks better than yesterday. How does it feel?" he asked.

"About the same. My whole arm hurts when I try to move. My nose also hurts, but last night, I tried to move it back into place. It actually feels better."

Titus examined her nose. It was still swollen, but he was able to gently move it between his thumb and finger. She grimaced and gasped. "I don't know how you handled the pain, but it seems like you got it back in place. I've got more medicine that will help with the pain, but try not to mess with your nose too much. It's still very swollen."

She nodded and leaned her head against the wall. Titus shifted his attention to her arm and blotted the skin around the open cut. "It really does look better, but it's a very deep wound. I'm going to add more ointment, so it's going to sting."

Livia yelped when the medicine touched her arm.

"I'm so sorry, Livia." Marius wiped her brow while inspecting the swelling around her nose and eye. "We'll try to work quickly."

"It's okay, Master. I know you are just trying to help."

They heard Clio cry out in pain, and Livia turned toward her. "She needs help, too," Livia implored.

"She's getting help, Livia. Justin and Jaalah are here, and they are helping her the way we are helping you."

Livia looked back at Marius and smiled. "Good, she needs them."

"Can you sit forward for me, so we can clean the wounds on your back?" Marius lifted her forward just like he had done the day before, and he held her while Titus cleaned the wounds and applied the oils and ointment. She cried out whenever Titus reached more sensitive wounds, but she was much stronger and much more alert than the day before.

When Titus finished, Marius gently adjusted the pillow at her back and eased her back against it.

She sighed when she was situated and placed her hand on his forearm. "Thank you, Master. Thank you for everything. Thank you for taking Cassia as your own. I'm so happy."

Marius' eyes widened, and his jaw dropped. "I think you misunderstood, Livia. I—"

"You mean you aren't going to take Cassia?" She cried and dug into his forearm. "Master, please. She needs you. I thought you . . . " She burst into tears, and through hiccups and sobs, she said, "Yours is the only home she's ever known. Please, Master. Please take care of Cassia."

Marius glanced at Titus and then toward Justin. He refused to be the cause of Livia's distress, so he cupped her face with his hands. "Hush, sweet Livia. I promise. I will take care of Cassia. I'll treat her as my own child, and she'll never want for anything ever again. I promise you, dear Livia."

He leaned back and opened his leather bag. "Look here." He pulled out the scrolls. "This is her manumission paper. Cassia is free. Look, Livia."

Livia glanced at the scroll, then back at Marius. "And you will take care of her, right?"

"Yes, Livia, I promise." Marius hated the pain in Livia's voice as she begged him to care for her child. He did not know how he would convince his mother, but he knew he would keep his promise to Livia, no matter the cost.

Titus prepared more opiates for Livia to drink, and they stayed long enough for her to eat a few bites of fruit and drink more water.

When the guard ordered the visitors to leave, Livia was calmer. She thanked Marius for promising to take Cassia and leaned back against the pillow with renewed peace.

When the group reached the carriage, Marius told Justin what Livia had said. "I don't exactly know how this will work. I don't know how I will handle my mother. She hates Cassia, and I fear that Cassia may not be safe with her. But I must figure it out because I promised Livia I would."

Justin placed his hand on Marius's shoulder and replied, "We can take it one day at a time. You can begin preparing for Cassia to return to your estate, but we'll keep her safe at our house until things are more stable."

Marius nodded. "Yes, yes, that's a good idea. I'll begin preparing at once, and we need to pray that Mother can accept the new order of things."

Marius grasped Justin's forearm, "Thank you, my friend. And now, I must prepare for my meeting with the governor."

"God go with you, my brother," Justin replied as they parted ways.

Once inside the carriage, Marius spent the entire ride home giving orders to Titus to prepare for Cassia's return—not as his slave, but as his daughter.

CHAPTER TWELVE

"This necklace is perfect for our dinner," Helena gushed, admiring her latest trinket. "Thank you for thinking of me." She touched the bright gemstones that hung in symmetrical rows around her neck. Her hair was lifted softly on each side with curled strands dangling prettily about her neck. A small, golden chain had been woven throughout the crown of her hair, and she had expertly applied subtle makeup to highlight her eyes and cheekbones. "Do I look satisfactory?" she asked apprehensively.

"Mother, look at me." When she obeyed, Marius continued. "There is not a woman in all of Nicomedia as lovely as you—nay, in all the empire. Calm yourself and let us enjoy our meal." Marius saw her pale cheeks flush under his compliment, and it did his heart good.

"You are a shameless flatterer to say such things to a woman my age. We both know you lie but thank you, anyway."

"Mother, it was you who taught me beauty is not just on the outside but that true beauty lies within."

He offered his arm, and when she placed her hand on his forearm, he led her to their carriage. He noted that she smelled faintly of jasmine and breathed deeply with a satisfied smile.

When they reached the palace, a beautifully landscaped path rich with fountains and statues led them to the main entrance. Handsomely clothed servants met them at grand steps, escorted them from their carriage, and led them through the courtyard. Heavy, marble columns surrounded them as they walked through the long corridor of the peristyle. Across the quadrangle, servants entered the hearth and returned with silver trays piled with rich delicacies.

At the end of the open hallway, they turned to their left and followed the stone walkway into the triclinium. Ornate carvings sat on elaborate pillars along each wall. Behind each couch, servants stood ready to serve them, and a lavish Roman feast was laid out before them. At each place sat one lettuce, three snails, two eggs, barley cake, and wine with honey. In the center of the table were olives, beetroots, gherkins, onions, and any number of fanciful truffles.

Pliny and his wife, Calpurnia, greeted them with utmost sincerity. "My young friend Marius, how kind of you to accept my invitation. And you, Mistress

Helena, look lovely this evening. Thank you for gracing our home."

"It is I who offers thanks to you, my lord, for your generous hospitality." Marius bowed low.

"Ah, you have saved me from a tiresome evening spent with my work. I have ordered a celebration for us to enjoy this night." He motioned for them to sit and clapped his hands to begin the meal.

Servants entered, carrying all manner of delicacies. Oysters, sow's innards, and sea urchins were placed before them; and the rich food induced lively conversation.

Marius sat amazed at his mother's transformation. Her elegance and grace were unmatched. She spoke cheerfully to each one at the table and charmed the governor and his wife throughout the meal. Her animated conversation awed Marius, who had almost imagined he would never see her laugh again, and he vowed to give her more opportunities to socialize.

Later in the evening, Pliny brought in a comic, who had them laughing gaily with his silly antics. As the sun set, servants brought delicate pastries and rich tartlets. While the group savored the sweet treats, a young singer serenaded them with her clear, smooth voice. The evening was a great delight to the young merchant, for his many months at sea did not allow him such pleasure often enough. The free and easy enjoyment calmed his anxious heart, and when Pliny finally shifted the conversation to the real reason for the meeting, Marius was prepared.

"Have you had your fill, Friend Marius?"

"Aye, my lord, I have had my fill and more."

"Then join me, if you will, in the bibliotheca." He stood and bowed to his wife and Mistress Helena. "Ladies, I trust you can entertain yourselves for a few moments while Marius and I have a more intimate visit."

With permission from the ladies, the men retreated to the bibliotheca further down the peristyle corridor. Marius was not prepared for the vast number of volumes, tablets, and scrolls that lined each wall. A large table sat in the center of the dark room, and the piles of papyrus spread across its surface indicated this was a place of refuge for the older man.

"Please, sit down, my friend. Would you like some wine?"

"No, my lord. I meant it when I said I've had my fill. You are a most generous host."

"Very well, then. Shall we discuss the matter of your slave?"

Marius appreciated his direct manner. It was somehow easier to approach him if the tone was kept businesslike. "Thank you, my lord. I wish very much to discuss her release."

"Her release? My boy, I do not think you understand her offense. I have personally questioned her, and she refuses to recant her Christian beliefs. I cannot allow such obstinacy to go unpunished."

Marius was undeterred, though it was not his own strength that made him so. He recognized immediately the hand of God in this discussion. "Sir, I have known this slave for more than fifteen years. Not once in that time has she shown even the smallest hint of disrespect or dishonor. In fact, I have observed such an opposite demeanor that it seemed nearly mystical. No matter what circumstance has clouded her life, this woman has evidenced tremendous calm and deep devotion to our family. I struggle deeply to see her demonstrate arrogant stubbornness."

Pliny sat across from Marius, his eyes studying him intently. "Then what do you call her refusal? She knows she will die, and Christians, by their very definition, deny any other deity but their own God. By denouncing the Roman way, they promote anarchy."

Marius knew well how to answer these questions, for he had struggled himself for many years with their complexities himself. "Like you, my lord, I, too, have wondered what it is that makes these Christians hold so firmly to their dangerous beliefs. I do not believe it is stubborn obstinacy but rather deeply held conviction that causes them to hold fast to their faith."

Pliny rubbed the back of his neck just below his sparse, gray hairline. When he looked at Marius, his words were sincere. "Aye, I admit the problem of Christians has perplexed me since I began my duties as proconsul. Even now. . . " He paused while rifling through a stack of papyrus in front of him. "Ah, here it is," he said, waving a particular document in Marius's direction. "Even now, I have been writing a letter to the emperor requesting assistance in the proper method of dealing with them. Like you, I have questioned enough of them to wonder at their faith. I admire loyalty and duty in anyone. Such conviction is rare amongst us these days. Yet I cannot condone a religion that freely promotes anarchy."

Marius knew this argument, too, for it was touted first by Nero and then every other leader since the earliest days following Christ's death. He spoke carefully, approaching the governor in the same way he, himself, had been approached with truth. "I have heard this, too, my lord, yet I found myself wondering at its truth. I have read some of their holy writings."

Marius noticed Pliny's raised brow, but he continued, undeterred. "In their writings, their God demands that they 'render . . . unto Caesar the things which are Caesar's.'[6] I have also read that they should be subject to their rulers and do good to them, obeying continually those in authority over them. They are even commanded to pray for their rulers and are told that these rulers are ministers of God. It seems rather inconsistent to suggest they are anarchists when they are commanded by their God to submit to their government."

Pliny listened intently. "I, too, have heard such things from their own lips, but what do you call it when one's religion demands that you obey your god above the emperor?"

"And yet that God demands reverent obedience to that same emperor?" Marius replied respectfully, continuing before Pliny could rebut. "Again, I use my eyes as much as my head to understand the seeming inconsistencies of this faith. A few years ago, I had never met a Christian—or rather, I had never met a

---

6 Matthew 22:21

Christian who publicly claimed their faith. Obviously, the family of slaves you have taken from our home are Christians I have known for years, but even they are a good example of my point."

He gained strength from the intent look in the governor's eyes. "Never have we had slaves who served us better. They work more faithfully than any other. They genuinely care for our needs more deeply than any other. They are more trustworthy and more dependable than any other, and it all speaks to their belief that they should wholeheartedly serve their God-given authority."

"Even in Rome, I met two Christian senators during this last visit. I questioned them intently. They believed unreservedly that it was their duty as Romans and as Christians to serve their country in such a way. Noblemen in Crete, fishermen in Greece, merchants in Rome, soldiers in Gaul, and slaves in my home all share one thing—their Christian faith— and that faith makes them greater servants to the empire than any other follower of any other religion our laws openly allow. Such a mystery required my investigation, my lord. I have spent much time researching this faith and studying its philosophies.

"Think of it, sir," he continued, words tumbling quickly out of his mouth. "If I am a soldier, I would want a man next to me who was not afraid to die—one who would stand the test of battle and do his job to the best of his ability. A true Christian does not fear death because he believes death unites him with his God."

"I certainly see your point, but does their morality allow them to kill? I seem to remember one stating it was against their belief to commit such a crime." The governor's questions were sincere, and Marius did not feel defensive.

"I, too, have read those passages in their holy writings. And in those same holy writings, their God gives the government not only the right but also the responsibility to bear the sword. Their writings seem to confirm that it is immoral to kill the innocent—that is to say, it is immoral to commit murder—but that one responsibility of a government is to protect its people, even by the use of the sword, if necessary.

"Furthermore, in the same passages that discuss the commandments against murder, authorities are once again commanded to take the life of a guilty man. I no longer see it as an inconsistency—simply a matter of well-defined terms." Marius shifted the conversation slightly. "Perhaps the example of the soldier confused my original point. You used to work in the treasury, sir. What kind of man is best qualified to do such an important task?"

Pliny nodded. "I see the point you are trying to make. You are implying that an honest man is better qualified because he is less likely to steal. And I assume you believe all Christians are honest men?"

"No, sir, I believe their doctrine states that there is no righteous man, not even one. I believe their doctrine states that even after one has converted to Christianity, he still fails to do what is right most every day. However, the difference is that because that failure displeases their God, they are more likely to change their behavior to align with those things that do please Him."

Pliny smiled. "I don't often see such passion for learning in the young men of our culture, my friend. It is truly refreshing. You seem to have a broad knowledge of these Christians. Yet I wonder, do you find it your duty to report them?"

He fumbled through the documents on his desk and lifted a small pamphlet, consisting of two sheets of papyrus folded in half and tied with hemp. "This booklet was recently given to me by a loyal Roman citizen, who felt it was his duty to report the names of all Christians known to him. What shall I do with it? What do you feel is your responsibility with the knowledge you have?"

Marius paled slightly, wondering if any of his new friends were listed in the pages of that book. Yet the Lord continued to give him courage to answer each question honestly. "I have not reported any of the Christians I know, for I do not see their faith as a crime against the empire. I asked the same question of my colleagues in the Senate, and they both implied that Trajan himself knows of their belief but does not consider them a threat."

He paused a moment, then thought of another man. "I cannot help but think of Herod Agrippa, who first served Emperor Claudius in Caesarea Philippi and then later near Jerusalem, when Titus Vespasianus successfully destroyed the city. As you may have heard, this great Roman leader requested an audience with a famed Christian leader; and after hearing his passionate discourse, Agrippa said he was nearly persuaded to become a Christian. If such a man as that can attest to the strengths of its tenets, I certainly cannot judge those who sincerely follow its doctrine."

Pliny studied Marius carefully. Marius knew very well that the governor's keen mind was not fooled by his passionate plea. Yet Pliny chose to continue the discussion.

"I admit that the Christians I have tried have not seemed to be overtly contrary to the government. In fact, almost every one of them claims to be a loyal citizen. The two slaves I have questioned this week talk of nothing more than a group of people who gather regularly to sing, read their holy writings, and pray. It seems innocent enough, yet every emperor since Nero has demanded their execution. Their threat to the empire has been obvious to more than one ruler. How do you explain that?"

"I cannot, sir. Nero's games, in my opinion, set a standard of cruelty that has never been duplicated and, I fear, will be recorded in history as a blot on our otherwise civil society. I do not consider his view of Christianity altogether unbiased, and there are those even within his own ranks who claim he is responsible for the fire that devastated Rome. Yet he blamed the Christians, whose tenets of morality condemned his lifestyle. It was, as you say, sir, Nero who first maintained their sect was dangerous to the empire. I find it somewhat suspect, at the very least."

Pliny's lips parted, and he made a slight but audible gasp at Marius' blunt statement. For a brief moment, he glared directly at Marius without a word. When Marius did not flinch, Pliny finally spoke.

"I have listened to all your arguments quite attentively, my friend. I cannot help but wonder if you, like Agrippa, have been persuaded by this sectarian religion?"

Marius glanced toward the floor, and for the first time since the conversation began, he felt his courage falter.

"My lord, I have read some of the greatest philosophers of our time. Like you, I have sat at the feet of men like Euphrates, the great stoic; Corellius Rufus; and others. When my father was alive, he thrived on the lively discussions of renowned men of learning. Like you, he has lined our family shelves with writings from great authors of every culture. I have read them all, and with those men, I have spent years searching for answers to my own questions about life and purpose. I cannot deny to you that in my quest to discover the tenets of Christianity, I have been converted to its doctrine."

When he finished, he found that his hands were shaking. He did not want to look at Pliny; but he knew he must learn his fate, so he dared to lift his eyes toward the powerful man across from him. Inwardly, he braced for a terrible doom.

Pliny did not speak. At first, he stared at Marius as if his ears had failed him. Then, he studied the little book in his hands. His eyes eventually fell upon the letter he was writing to the emperor.

When he finally spoke, his tone was warm. "Unlike you, my friend, I am not at liberty to excuse this sect without authority from the emperor. I am subject to his command. However, I am an old man, and I consider myself a genial devotee to true reform. I am open to new ideas, and I admit that the peace I see in your eyes is attractive to me. Perhaps, I will study this sect more carefully and read its documents for myself. It is how I would handle any other new philosophy, so it is only fair that I give Christianity the same examination."

He reached for his reed pen, dipped it in ink, and scrawled something on the back of the pamphlet. "Since I find no sign of anarchy in the two slave women I have taken, I will release them into your capable hands on the morrow. You may retrieve them from the prison in the morning after nine o'clock."

He dipped the pen into the ink again and wrote several lines outlining his orders on a piece of fresh papyrus. When he was finished, he rolled the document into a scroll, then used a candle to melt a stick of bright red wax. Once it softened, he dripped a small amount onto the scroll and used his ring to make an impression onto the seal. Then he handed the scroll to Marius and warned, "Understand, though, if the emperor directs me to take other action, I must comply with his command."

"I understand, my lord, and thank you for your mercy." Marius rose, crossed the room, and knelt before the proconsul. He kissed the ring on the elder man's outstretched hand and waited for further instruction.

"Rise, my boy. You need not thank me so. Nor must you fear retribution from me, for I see a great change in you. Your confidence is contagious, and I envy your peace."

Marius rose. "It was the peace I saw in others that led me to their Savior, my lord. It is available to you as well."

"Aye, it is good of you to concern yourself with my wellbeing, son; but alas, I have spent my life worshipping the gods of my fathers, and they have not failed me. It has saddened me to see their deserted temples and to see so many turn away from the sacred rites. Now, as I see the sale of sacrificial animals slowly rise again, I have hopes that many Christians like yourself—" He paused with a mirthful twinkle in his eyes. "—could be reformed if given the chance to repent. While I do not agree with your evaluation of this sect—for I see it, at the very least, as a dangerous and repulsive cult—I do respect you. And though I jest about your repentance, I pray to my gods that you do."

Marius bowed, wishing to say more, but the governor had risen, indicating that the conversation was done. The governor motioned toward the door, and when they reached the corridor of the peristyle, he paused and asked, "What does your mother think of your conversion?"

Marius's cheeks flushed with shame. "She does not yet know. It is quite a new development, and as she has been so distraught over the week's events, I have not told her."

"I am surprised, my friend. If this religion offers what you claim, would you not enthusiastically share it with everyone, especially those you love the most?"

"Yes, my lord. It is as you say. I want more than anything to give her the same hope I have, but to my great shame, I have been reluctant because of her noted opposition to it. However, I intend to speak with her this very evening and tell her of my conversion. Whether she will listen, I cannot say."

Pliny grinned. "It would be very frightening, indeed, to displease such a pleasant woman. May your God go with you."

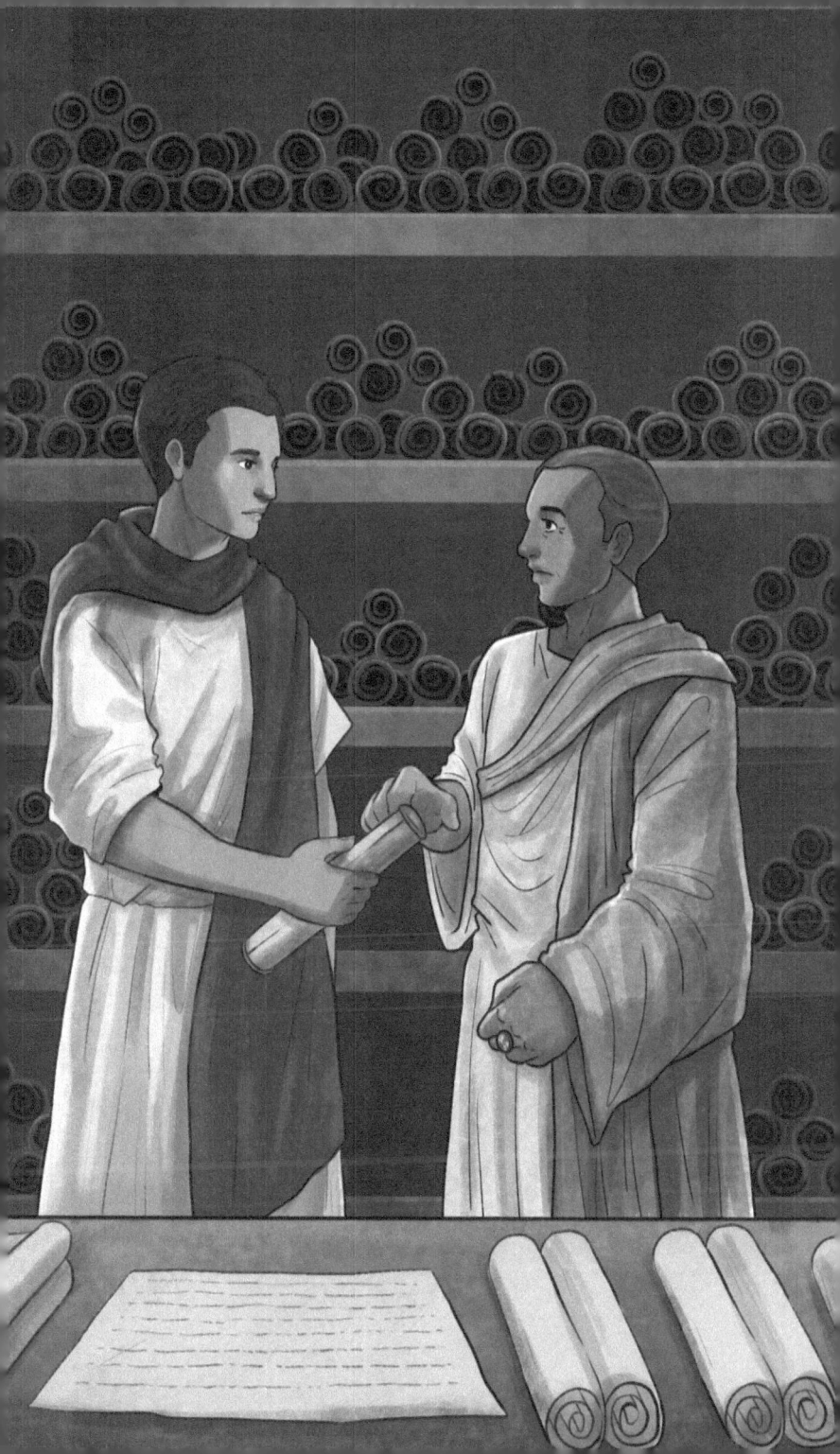

Marius laughed. "It would indeed, my lord. And thank you again for your assistance tonight."

"Think not of it again, my friend, and perhaps we can meet again and discuss our different philosophies."

"I look forward to it."

Chapter Thirteen

"It was a lovely evening, wasn't it, my son?"

"It certainly was, Mother. I cannot remember when I've enjoyed myself so much. The governor is truly a noble man who has mastered the art of hospitality. And, Mother, if I may say so, your beauty, charm, and elegance added much to the evening. I'm so glad you came. I want us to have many more dinner parties with our friends. It made you so happy."

Helena smiled, absently twisting her new necklace. Without warning, her eyes pooled, and a single tear coursed unheeded down her pale cheek. Marius rose to sit next to her. The jarring carriage nearly dumped him into her lap, and they both laughed despite the tenseness of the moment.

"Please don't cry, Mother. I want you to be so happy."

She clasped his hands in her own and lifted them to her lips. He wiped her tear, and the gesture brought a surge of them. She leaned against his chest, trying to fight the emotion, but the sobs tore from her like a rushing river cascading over a steep waterfall.

"I have . . . so much . . . to tell you." She sobbed between words. "I've needed . . . you so much . . . and you haven't been here."

"Shhh, Mother. I'm here now, and I, too, have much to tell you." He lifted a loose strand of her hair and clumsily tucked it back into the jeweled comb behind her ear. He spoke loud enough to be heard over the roar of the wheels against the gravelly road, yet his voice was gentle. "I first want to ask for your forgiveness. I've hurt for so long, and I've searched for peace and shut myself off from you and this place. I'm so sorry I haven't been here for you. I am ashamed of my failures, but I want you to know that I'm not leaving you again."

Her head jerked up at his words, and she studied his face. "What are you saying?"

"I'm saying that I am no longer going to captain any of our ships. I will not be leaving you. I will not be spending the sailing ban in another port. I will not be a part-time son anymore."

"But how is that possible? What about the business?"

Marius laughed, and his voice was light. "Mother, listen to me; Father handpicked most of our captains long ago, and they have faithfully served us for years. They are much more qualified than I've ever been, and I have worked closely with each one. I trust them as much as Father did. They are good men who know their trade, and they have more influence with merchants in each port than I'll ever have. They have learned to trust me, too, for I have been very generous whenever they have succeeded. I will simply remain here and oversee all the cargo acquisitions and disbursements. The fact is, I don't want to leave anymore. What do you say to that? Do you think you can stand having me around all the time?"

"Oh, my son, you have no idea how sweet your words are to me. I'm so . . . happy." Her voice faded as fresh tears began to fall, and she once again buried her head against his chest. For many moments, they rode in silence.

He rested his cheek on the top of her head and offered many quiet prayers of thanksgiving for all the miracles of the evening. He also prayed for the wisdom and courage to tell his mother of his salvation and of his plans for Livia and Cassia. He half-smiled, realizing he was more afraid of her than he had been of Proconsul Pliny.

They were nearing their country home when Mother sat up and wiped her eyes. "Marius," she said, her voice almost a whisper. "I told you I had something to tell you, and your words tonight have been like medicine to me." He waited for her to continue, but she seemed to be struggling. With a mild shrug of her shoulders, she finally blurted out, "I'm sick."

She tried to smile, but the furrows on her forehead and the way she rubbed her temples gave him a graphic picture of the pain she was in.

"What do you mean you're sick?" Marius was immediately alarmed. He turned his body to face her directly and grabbed both of her thin hands. "Mother, I . . . what are you saying?" But he saw it in her eyes. He barely heard her words.

"The doctors all agree that I only have a few more months—maybe a year, but . . . " She trailed off, her brave front collapsing in another rush of sorrow.

"No, oh, please, God, no. Don't take her from me. Not now. Please, God."

As he prayed, her body stiffened. She slowly pulled away from him, and when she turned her questioning eyes to his, he realized what he'd done.

"What did you just say?" She studied him a moment longer and watched as he fumbled for the right words. "Were you just . . . *praying*?" She pushed away from him, total disgust painted across her puffy face.

Just then, the carriage stopped, and Phinneus opened the door. He offered a hand to Helena and steadied her while she dismounted the narrow step. Marius jumped down behind her and called her name, but she nearly ran through the courtyard and disappeared beneath the arched door. He noticed Phinneus' expression, but his faithful scrvant wisely held his tongue.

"I trust all my orders have been carried out," Marius asked instead.

"Yes, my lord. The room is prepared. Titus delivered the clothing this evening, and the servants have been given their assignments. They are settled into their quarters, but I can call them if you wish to speak to them."

"No, I will speak to them in the morning. Has Titus already left?"

"Yes, my lord. About an hour ago."

Marius frowned and quickly reevaluated his plan. He realized, as he mentally made a list of what needed to be done, how very small his faith had been. If he had trusted God from the beginning, he would be well-prepared for Livia's return. As it was, he had only prepared for Cassia. Phinneus stood nearby, quietly awaiting instructions.

"Prepare the other guestroom as well. Make sure it is as comfortable as possible. First thing in the morning, I want you to deliver a message to Titus.

Tomorrow will be very busy, and I will need more help. However, until we can arrange that, speak to Caecilia and see that she is ready to serve. Have her prepare healing salves and balms, for they will surely be needed."

When he was finished with Phinneus, he darted into the villa and nearly ran down the corridor to his mother's room. When he neared the door, he heard her tears, and his heart broke.

Oh, Lord, please soften her heart and draw her to You. She needs You so much.

He tapped lightly on the door, then entered her freshly cleaned chamber. Her body was draped across the bed, her head buried in her hands. Without looking up, she cried, "Please . . . tell me you are . . . not . . . one of *them*."

He knelt beside the bed, raised her head from her hands, and waited while she shifted to a sitting position. He straightened pillows around her back, then sat on the edge facing her. "We are going to talk about some things tonight, Mother. It may take us the rest of the night, but we cannot go another day without resolving many things. I am your son, and I love you. I want to know about your illness, and I want to find the best physicians in the empire to help us fight it."

"Hush, Marius. I do not want to discuss my illness." Her voice was harsh, and it was clear she had again retreated behind the unyielding walls of her heart. "Tell me." Her voice broke, but her eyes held his. He reached for her hands, but she yanked them away. "Tell me," she demanded again.

"I am what you fear, Mother. I have become a Christian."

"Get out." She pushed frantically against him. "Get out, and don't you ever come back to this house. Get away from me."

She beat against his chest, striking blow after blow after blow, but he refused to budge. Tears flowed from his eyes as he watched her fight against the thing that had become dearer to him than life itself.

Oh, God, help her see You. Break through the bitterness and hatred and help her. Please, help her, God.

"I love you, Mother. I love you more than anything. Please listen to me." Over and over, he begged, but she refused to listen. When her energy was finally spent, she fell against him, cursing his very being. Her words cut him more deeply than any blade ever could.

"How could you? How could you convert to the one thing I hate most and still claim that you love me?"

"It is because I love you that I want to tell you. You must listen to me. You do not need to fear

Christianity, Mother. Many of your dearest friends have also found this peace. Senators Rex and Luciano have uncompromising faith in Jesus Christ. They have forsaken the gods that forsook them and have turned to the one God Who has never failed them. Friend Decimus in Crete and Friend Primius in Troas—all of them have been converted as I have."

"Hush. I said I don't want to hear it. You will bring destruction on this household. If the proconsul ever finds out—"

"He already knows, and he—"

"He knows?" She didn't let her son finish. "You have brought our doom, you fool."

"Please, hear me. Not only does the proconsul know that I am a Christian, but he has also assured me that I will not face retribution. He is studying its tenets for himself and has agreed to release Livia because he can find no fault in her."

Helena's mouth opened as if to rebut his words, but she just sat with her jaw open, staring wide-eyed at his declaration. "W-what exactly are you saying?"

He reached for her hand again, and this time, she did not pull away. "I'm saying that the days of Nero are gone. Rome is no longer afraid to discover a faith whose followers live with such conviction they would rather die than deny it. Rome is discovering that the tenets of this faith are neither dangerous nor anarchist. Rome is opening its eyes to the truth of the Holy Scriptures, and when faced with that truth, Rome is opening its heart to the Savior, Who offers peace to their souls.

"Mother, look around you. Haven't you noticed how deserted the temples have become? Haven't you seen the empty shops that once thrived selling sacrificial flesh? Nothing but Truth could change a society so quickly; and nothing but Truth could sweep across every class, tribe, and tongue. If you would but open your eyes, you would see the glorious light of the Gospel, and it would soothe your troubled spirit. Oh, if you would just open your heart and let the Savior heal your soul."

He pleaded with her for many minutes, but she was not ready. However, when he kissed her gently on the forehead, he could see a softening; and he prayed out loud, "Lord, you have given me the dearest mother, and I love you for it. She's hurting so much, and I know you can help. Please tear down the walls of her heart and help her see her need of You. I love her so much, dear Lord, and I want her to have the same peace that floods my heart."

She stared at him, clearly both shocked and touched by his words, but she remained silent.

"Sleep well. We will discuss other matters in the morning." When he rose, she held his hand a moment longer.

"I love you, Marius."

He was confounded as his heart tried to mingle all of the emotions of the last few hours. On the one hand, it was all he could do not to shout his praises to God for the miracle He worked in allowing Livia to be released. He punched his right fist into his left palm and nearly cried, "Hallelujah." But as he entered his bedchamber, he was also overcome with grief. His dear mother was sick, and she was not ready for eternity. The stress of confessing his salvation to both the proconsul and his mother in the span of one evening still affected him. His mother's reaction cut him deeply, but her softening in the last few minutes gave him hope. He dropped to his knees and released it all to God.

A storm outside came and went, but Marius Luciano never knew. He was so deep in prayer that even the terrible tempest could not move him.

CHAPTER FOURTEEN

Marius waited on the bench outside his mother's room early the next morning. As soon as he heard her movement, he knocked on her door. When she called her greeting, he entered expectantly, hoping for the same softness from the night before. She sat on her couch, running Julia's necklace through her fingers. Without looking up, she spoke.

"If your God is so loving, why did He take them from us?"

He walked to the window and placed a kiss on her forehead, then studied her vacant eyes. They were bloodshot and drawn. He sat beside her, placed his hand on her forearm, and gently tried to share his faith.

"I cannot lie, Mother. I do not always understand His ways. I don't have all the answers. I don't know why God took our family from us. But I do know that He loves us, and I know that He is good. He is always good. No matter how much I hated Him and no matter how far I ran from Him, He found me. And by His grace, He saved me."

She slid her arm from underneath his caress and arose, the familiar coldness overtaking her demeanor. She wrapped the necklace around her wrist, doubling the chain to secure it like a bracelet, then spoke, enunciating each sound in a haughty tone. "You said we had more matters to discuss?"

Her frosty tone and candid questions discouraged him. The softening he had witnessed last night was gone. However, he respected her mood and rising from the bench, he answered frankly.

"The proconsul is releasing Livia this morning. I am having her and her daughter brought back here. I . . . " He knew his next words would shatter her composure, and he hesitated.

"Go on."

He turned away and paced, eventually resting on the stone bench on the far side of the room. "I will be . . . I plan to . . . " He sat forward, resting his elbows and forearms on his thighs and dropped his head. "I want Livia and Cassia to live with us—not as our slaves, but as our family."

He glanced at Helena and noticed that her entire body tensed; but she did not speak, so he continued. "I have granted them both manumission, and by law, they are now full Roman citizens. They have the same rights and responsibilities as anyone else. I want to treat them as such." His mouth was dry.

"Am I to understand that I have no say in this?" Her voice was tight and high-pitched.

He didn't reply. He sat studying the leather cuffs around his wrists, and she stared blankly at the blossoms outside her window.

"Is that all?"

His voice was soft, but firm. "I want them to . . . to join our family."

When she turned her eyes on him, they were blazing. They started out opened wide, and then narrowed in consternation. "I'll not have any part of this, Marius. I won't."

His shoulders drooped. Tears pooled around the rims of his eyes, and when he rose, defeat was evident. "I love you, Mother. I want this more than anything, but I also want your consent."

He grasped her hands and locked his eyes on hers. She did not flinch, so he dropped her hands and stated, "I'm retrieving Livia from the prison this morning. She's been badly beaten and flogged and will need significant care. I've had the servants prepare the guestroom for her to use while she recovers."

He glanced at her again and noted the hard set of her jaw. Without another word, she walked away.

On Marius' way to the carriage, he checked Livia's room. Phinneus had arranged everything perfectly. Fresh flowers sat in a basket on a shelf; bread and fruit were neatly displayed on a silver platter. Two large basins filled with water sat ready for use; and an array of linen cloth, oils, and medicines were organized on the table beside the bed. Satisfied, he left the villa, climbed into the carriage, and rode into town. He saw nothing of the countryside nor heard the beautiful sounds of nature awakening after such a dreadful storm. He closed his eyes and drifted into a restless sleep.

When he arrived at the carpenter's shop to meet Justin, he was groggy and disoriented; but when he saw Cassia in her fresh, white tunica and simply braided hair, his heart leaped. He had sent word earlier with the details surrounding the release of the women, and he could see pure joy on each face as they loaded into the carriages and headed to the prison.

Cassia, who had never ridden in a carriage before, kept stroking the deep crimson cushions and tracing the gold-brocaded trim.

Marius knew at once he could never turn her out, for he loved this child as if she were his very own. *Lord, please reach Mother's heart. Help her see how much this child has to give. Ease her sorrow. Open her heart. Last night, You moved the heart of the proconsul. I'm asking You today to melt the heart of my dear mother.*

The carriage circled around to the east side of the palace and continued beyond the beautifully carved stone walls surrounding the courtyard. At the end of a long row, they turned sharply, and the landscape changed. They reached another gate, one with less ornamented adornment, and slowly moved through its simple stone archway.

"What's that building?" Cassia asked, staring at the large, but simple, stone edifice.

"That is the basilica. It is where your mother was tried."

"It seems scary," she said as they drove past.

"It can be, but it is also the place where the innocent are set free."

She grinned again. "I like it."

Both Titus and Marius laughed. Her childlike view of life was refreshing, and Marius' spirit revived a little.

They rounded the basilica and followed a narrower road toward the prisons. The harsh terrain was a stark contrast to the serene grounds through which they had just passed. When they reached the gate, Marius descended the carriage and presented himself to the guard. He handed over the sealed scroll and waited while the document was reviewed.

Cassia, her face peering through the window opening, began trembling with hope. Marius smiled, trying to calm her nerves; and when the guard motioned for him to enter, he winked, causing her to flush.

Leaving Cassia to wait in the carriage under their driver's care, Marius, Titus, and Justin followed a soldier through the dismal passageway into the desolate quadrangle. They followed the guard to the cell just like they had done before, and when the guard finally opened the lock, Marius bolted into the cell and crossed to Livia's side.

She smiled, and he knelt next to her holding her hand. "You won't believe what's happened, Livia! Oh, darling, you've been set free!"

Other than a slight nod, she didn't react. "Livia, do you understand, you've been set free!" She smiled again but didn't speak.

Titus removed the blanket from her shoulders and reached behind her to get the pillow. He gathered the oil lamp and put all of the supplies into the basket, and still Livia never spoke.

Marius cupped her face and leaned in so she could see him better. Her skin was hot, and sweat beaded her brow. He quickly grabbed the water, poured some onto a cloth, and dabbed her forehead. Then he poured small droplets into her mouth. "Livia, can you hear me? Are you still with me? Come now, try to drink."

Her eyes closed, and she leaned her head against the wall. He patted her face. "No, darling, stay with me."

He poured the water onto her neck, and she opened her eyes again. Her body shivered, and she seemed to be breathing heavily.

"I'm so tired," she whispered.

He knelt close and whispered, "You'll be home soon; just stay with me."

The guard came then and clumsily grabbed the shackle on her leg. She groaned, and Marius turned his ire onto the soldier. "Be more careful. Haven't you made her suffer enough?"

The guard ignored him and continued to fiddle with the locks on each shackle. Marius turned toward Justin and saw that he had already carried Sister Clio to the gate. Titus was gathering the final supplies, and Marius nearly burst with anger at the guard who was taking so long to set Livia free.

When the guard grabbed her wounded arm, she screamed. Marius roared at the guard, "Stop, you're hurting her." And when the guard loosened the final shackle, Marius pulled Livia into his arms and turned her away from her tormentor.

He carried her out of that miserable pit and climbed each step whispering encouragement to her. "We're almost there; just hold on a few more minutes. Soon, it will be over."

When they reached the top and he saw her in the full light of day, he was overcome with compassion. This woman that he so dearly loved had suffered greatly behind these walls. He vowed that as long as he lived and as much as was in his power to stop it, she would never suffer like this again.

By the time he reached the courtyard, he could see Justin far ahead of him placing Clio into a carriage loaned to them by a member of their church. Marius realized that Clio was as broken, gaunt, and pale as Livia was; and he was sickened by the treatment that Rome imposed on its enemies.

When he passed the guards, they sneered, showing their disgust at Livia's stench. Marius was furious but managed to maneuver past them toward the final exit of the quadrangle.

The first guard stopped him and held out another sealed scroll. "The proconsul insisted I give this to you."

The disgusted look on Marius' face must have intimidated the guard because he stated, "I'll just slip it into your pouch there." He shoved the scroll into Marius' leather pouch and stood aside.

As quickly but carefully as he could, Marius walked out of the gate and toward the carriage. His first glimpse of Cassia would be imprinted in his heart forever. She stood with her hands on the frame of the window, jumping up and down. Tears coursed down her face, and one stray strand of dark brown hair bounced gaily in rhythm as she moved. He heard her joyous squeals over and over. "Mother, Mother, Mother."

Titus, who had gone on ahead of Marius, reached the carriage first and opened the door. Cassia jumped from the carriage and ran toward Marius. She tried to put a hand on the frail frame of her dear mother, but Marius cautioned her, "Step back, Cassia; we need to get your mother in the carriage immediately."

Cassia obeyed, but as she surveyed the bloodied garments and bruised face of her mother, she burst into tears.

Brother Justin came up behind her and lifted her in his arms. "Cassia, I warned you that she was badly beaten, but this is a time to rejoice. Her wounds will heal, but we can rejoice that she is free."

In his typical fashion, Brother Justin began talking to God. "Thank You, dear Savior, for this miracle." Emotion choked his voice as he continued, "You've brought our sisters home. You are our great Hope, and Your mercy is great."

Marius lifted Livia into the carriage, and Titus helped get her settled on the seat. Marius sat next to her, his arm around her practically holding her up. Cassia knelt on the floor with her head buried in her mother's lap, and they both wept. Marius offered Livia more water to drink, while Titus wiped cool rags across the wound on her arm. The jolts of the carriage significantly hampered their work, but by the time they reached Justin's home, they were ready to rejoice with their Christian brothers and sisters. And the rejoicing was great.

Piles of food covered every surface. Some sang favorite hymns, while others offered prayers of thanksgiving. The women tended to the wounds of each prisoner with gentle care and expensive salves. And every worker, every caregiver, and every well-wisher had to accomplish their tasks around the little maid Cassia, for she would not leave her mother's side. They all gladly accommodated the interference, for they were greatly stirred by the blessed reunion of mother and child.

CHAPTER FIFTEEN

It was late afternoon before Marius felt that Livia was able to withstand the journey to his villa. Titus called for the carriage, and they carefully lifted Livia into the compartment. The women from the church had cleaned her wounds. She was in a new tunica, and her hair had been braided and pinned into a simple bun at the nape of her neck. Marius placed the back of his hand on her forehead and still thought her skin felt hot, but she was much revived from when he had first removed her from the prison.

She rested her head against his shoulder, and Cassia resumed her place on the floor and placed her hands on Livia's. Livia slept most of the way to the villa and barely awoke when Marius carried her from the carriage to her room.

Phinneus had readied a bath, and a physician stood ready to assess her wounds. Cassia, her little hand clutching her mother's tunica, refused to leave until Marius persuaded her.

"Come here, child. I have something to tell you."

When she obeyed, he knelt beside her and whispered, "I have prepared a very special evening for your mother. I have brought in an important doctor to help her feel better, and I have many servants who need to get her even more cleaned up than she already is. I promise when we are done getting her all ready, you can return and spend the rest of the evening with her. Is that fair?"

Cassia nodded. Marius took her hand and led her from the room, allowing the physician to examine Livia without disturbing the young child. They walked down the corridor to the very next room, and when they entered, she gasped. "This is so pretty; look at all the flowers."

"I'm glad you like it, Cassia, for it is yours. From now on, you are the lady of this room. And all ladies need maids, so I want to introduce you to yours." He nodded for the two servants to approach and gave them their instructions. "Cassia, this is Anna and Fabia. I believe you already know them, right?"

She nodded, and he continued, "They will prepare to look your very best for when you see your mother later."

She seemed confused, but he was not deterred. "I want you to look pretty for your mother. I don't want her to be sad about the time you were apart, and I don't want her to worry about how you fared. Let's show her that you were well cared for and help calm her heart."

He knew that Cassia would do anything to ease her mother's burdens, and he was not surprised when she eagerly agreed. He had already instructed the servants to keep Cassia occupied for several hours so that Livia could be privately attended to. He expected that Cassia's preparations would be quite foreign to her, so he motioned for her to join him on the low couch beneath the window.

"Cassia, do you remember what I told you about our family?"

She nodded. "Yes, Master. I am no longer your slave, but I am your daughter."

"That's right. And you've never been my daughter before. So, it's going to be very different for you now. But I want you to try really hard to act like my daughter. Can you do that?"

"I think so."

"Good. The first way you can start is to let Anna and Fabia serve you. It might seem strange, but I want you to trust them and do what they say today. They took care of my little girl, and they know just what to do. Can you do that for me?"

Cassia nodded and looked shyly at the two servants standing by the large tub. Anna was young and often worked with Livia, so Cassia seemed very comfortable with her. But Fabia was old, and Cassia looked nervous when she glanced toward the older woman.

Marius noticed her hesitation and put his hand on Cassia's. "Fabia helped me when I was your age, Cassia. I've known her my whole life."

Cassia looked into Marius's eyes and nodded. "I'll do what they say, Master."

"I know you will, but I know it's going to be hard. So, I've got one more surprise for you." He nodded toward the door. When Cassia followed his gaze, she saw Sister Jaalah.

She jumped up and ran to her, and Jaalah simply hugged her. "You don't think I'd let you have all this fun without me, do you?" she asked the child.

Marius could see that Cassia was in good hands, so he bowed to Jaalah and quietly exited the room. He knew he needed to speak to his mother but dreaded the confrontation.

He found her in her room in a sullen mood. He pretended to pat the dust off of his tunic before starting the unpleasant conversation; but Helena was ready to pounce. Before he could even cross the room to kiss her, she immediately exclaimed, "I will have nothing to do with this, Marius. Get those two out of my house."

"Mother, please be reasonable," he pleaded. They have done nothing wrong. They have been faithful to our family and—"

"We can't risk having them here." Stubbornly, Helena turned her back on her son.

He tried to reason with her, but in a moment of utter frustration, he grabbed his mother's arm and turned her toward him.

"You are coming with me, Mother," he demanded.

When she refused, he put his arm around her waist and forcibly guided her out of her room. She resisted until he said, "I'll carry you if I have to, but you are going to join me one way or another."

She turned her eyes on him and spat out, "Is this what I am to expect from the new *Christian* Marius? Is this my new son?"

The venom in her question cut him deeply, but he still forced her to go with him.

He dragged her to Livia's room. When they arrived, Livia was stretched out on the bed, facedown. Her back and legs were shredded by the flogging she had received. The doctor was bent over her gently applying salve to each open wound, and Caecilia was on her knees in front of Livia holding her hand and stroking her head as Livia cried out in pain.

"Look at her, Mother. Just look at her."

Helena gasped and cried out, "Take me away from here, Marius."

Marius took her back to her room but lectured her the entire way. "That woman has served you more faithfully than any other slave in our home. She has loved you and cared for you in your darkest hours. When Aurelia died, Livia saved our Julia by nursing her in her infancy. When Julia and Father died, you told me yourself it was Livia who gave you the most comfort."

Reaching Helena's room, Marius released his grip on her. In disgust, he continued his tirade. "I always thought you were the most loving and kind woman. I've loved you, laughed with you, hurt with you, and cried with you. You are my mother, and I love you. But I cannot understand how you can be so vile and unfeeling as to so easily abandon your affections of those you claim to love. First you denounce Livia, and now you denounce me. And for what? Just because we have a different belief than you? That belief is what made Livia love you so faithfully. If you can hate someone as kind and loving as Livia, then shame on you, Mother!"

Marius shook his head and began to turn from his mother. "I *am* a new Marius, and I've got a lot to learn about being a Christian. But the one thing I have figured out is that loving people is more important than playing games and building façades to impress people who don't care about anything more than your wealth."

He gestured toward her door. "In those rooms down the hall are two people who deserve our compassion if for nothing more than the many years they have faithfully served us.

"And let me just add that they have served you with love even when you have behaved reprehensibly toward them. I know all about your treatment of Cassia. She's just a child, Mother. What has happened to you? If I lose a few aristocratic friends by loving such beautiful souls, then so be it. But so help me, Mother, I will not abandon them in their greatest hour of need. And if you choose to discard me as your son because of that, then that is your burden to carry."

He stomped from the room and went back to tend to his new family.

Cassia laughed. Fabia was telling her the story of Porcus the pig.

"Porcus started grunting as soon as I opened the gate. When he nudged my legs, I fell backward and landed on my bottom. The entire bowl of slop landed all over me, and Porcus just came on over and began licking it right off my belly."

By the time Fabia finished her story, Cassia and Sister Jaalah were laughing out loud. "I'll tell you what, I don't think that pig even realized he was a pig. But when I got back to the servant's quarters that day, I scrubbed myself until I hurt. It wasn't a fancy bath like this one you're getting, but it worked."

"Whatever happened to Porcus?" Cassia asked.

"Come here, child." Fabia turned her face away and closed her eyes while she held a large towel wide between her arms."

Cassia glanced at Sister Jaalah and Anna, who also had their faces turned away and their eyes closed. She exited the tub of water and walked into the cloth while Fabia wrapped it around her. Once she was safely covered, Fabia continued her story while patting Cassia dry.

"Well, I'll tell you. A few years later, Porcus was getting too old to be much use to anyone. So,

Mistress Helena ordered that he be served for a very great and special celebration."

"She did what?" Cassia's eyes widened and she grabbed at her chest in horror. "You mean she *ate* him?"

"Well, yes, child. What do you think we do with pigs?"

Cassia shook her head. "Poor Porcus."

"Oh, but Porcus served his purpose, child," the old maid continued. "And do you know what special feast he helped us all celebrate?"

Cassia just shook her head glumly.

"Mistress Helena served that pig at the feast she prepared to celebrate your mama and papa's wedding."

Cassia's head jerked up, and a tiny grin formed.

Fabia continued, "That old, ugly, hairy Porcus got to give us all great joy. We got to celebrate your mama and papa with some of the tastiest meat I can ever remember eating."

Sister Jaalah leaned in. "It just goes to show you, doesn't it, that we never know who God will use to help us. But even in what may seem like sad things, God is still able to give us joy."

Cassia nodded and smiled. "I get it now. It's like what you were telling me about Governor Pliny. I didn't want to pray for him. I didn't want God to do anything nice for him. But God used him to give me back my mama. I wouldn't have wanted Porcus to die, but God used Porcus to help everyone celebrate Mother and Father."

Jaalah laughed. "Something like that, my dear." She put her arm around Cassia's shoulder and squeezed her. "You know what else God has done for you, Cassia?"

Cassia looked up and shook her head.

Jaalah smiled. "Only about an hour ago, you were frightened and feeling alone. Now, you've made great friends with Fabia and Anna, and you know that they will care for you just the way the master planned."

Cassia shyly lowered her head but glanced up at Fabia. The older woman winked at her, and she grinned. "I guess the master knows best," she whispered.

For the rest of the afternoon, Anna and Fabia prepared Cassia. After they bathed her in a tub filled with sweet-smelling rose petals, they placed a new robe on her shoulders. Then Anna rubbed lavender-scented oils into her feet, calves, hands, and arms. The massage was the most luxurious thing Cassia had ever experienced, and she was sad when it was over.

Next, they used a small reed tool to gently scrape away the excess oils, and the tingling sensation was immensely relaxing. By the time they were ready to dress her, she was almost asleep. Anna placed her feet in new sandals. Each sandal had tiny jewels dangling from the straps that wrapped up her legs. She turned them often to watch them glimmer. When Fabia retrieved her tunica from the shelf, Cassia sucked in her breath.

"It's beautiful," she sighed. The soft, white material was trimmed in gold; and when they dressed her, she felt like an empress.

At last, they fixed her hair. Standing on each side of her, Anna and Fabia placed a drizzle of olive oil in their palms and then rubbed it into her scalp and down to the ends of her hair. Then, using heated rods, they twisted strands so they dangled prettily about her face. They lifted her curls atop her head and held them firmly in place with beaded combs. Fabia expertly wove tiny pearls and flowers throughout each strand.

When Cassia was ready, she gave them warm and lingering hugs. Then, she grabbed Sister Jaalah's hand, and they went to the triclinium to await Master Marius.

CHAPTER SIXTEEN

Marius entered the triclinium, and without a word, Cassia ran to him and threw her arms around his waist. With her head tilted upward, she whispered, "I love you, Master."

His throat was tight. He could not tear his eyes from her face. Looking at her transformation, he determined to reward Anna and Fabia. The heavy scent of lavender would always bring him back to this moment.

"I love you, too, Cassia." The words came easily, as if he'd said them to her a hundred times; but it was not lost on him that, in fact, this was the first time he had told his new child of his love.

Before she released him, Caecilia entered the room. "Maid Livia is ready, Master."

He turned to Cassia. "Are you ready to go see your mother?" Cassia quickly nodded.

Marius had checked on Livia many times throughout the afternoon, and each time, she was sleeping deeply. The doctor had given her strong opiates to help her sleep while he worked to clean her wounds. They had also bathed her and massaged oils into her skin, much like Anna and Fabia had done to Cassia. Caecilia had readied Livia with a simple tunica and braid. The bath, rest, and opiates did much to restore Livia's stability.

When Cassia and Marius arrived, Livia was propped up in bed, leaning against several well-placed cushions. Her wounded arm had been bandaged with strips of linen cloth and lay across her lap. The cuts and bruises on her face and the swelling around her eye were still appalling, but Marius thought she had never looked more beautiful.

His lips parted; his heart quickened; and his breathing became strangely shallow. "Livia." He breathed her name reverently. Cassia dropped his hand and ran to the bed.

"Mother. I barely recognize you." Cassia tried to hug Livia and did not see the slight grimace of pain, but Marius did. He quickly pulled a chair close to the bed and suggested that Cassia sit so they could be careful of Livia's wounds. Livia's smile showed her gratitude.

"Oh, Cassia, my darling. I barely recognize you either. Stand back and let me look at you."

Cassia moved away from the bed and then twirled around, while grabbing the sides of her tunica. "Isn't it beautiful, Mother?"

"Oh, yes, Cassia. I've never seen anything so beautiful." Livia wiped at her eyes, and Jaalah quickly grabbed a cloth and helped her dab away the tears of joy.

"Thank you, Jaalah," Livia whispered. "I'm so glad you are here."

Jaalah squeezed her shoulder and then stepped back so that Cassia could get closer.

While Cassia and Livia talked, Marius prayed. He loved them both. He wanted to marry Livia, but he knew that doing so would deeply hurt his mother, whom he also loved.

Suddenly, he struggled to breathe. He knew he needed to make things right with Helena. He knew he needed to admit his sin against her, but his own stubbornness kept him from rushing to her room. The prompting of the Holy Spirit weighed upon him, but he refused to respond.

"Don't you think, Master?" Cassia's question brought him back to the present.

"I'm sorry. What did you say, child?"

"Don't you think my new sandals are pretty?" She had lifted her foot up on the bed to show Livia her sandals, and she proudly displayed them for him to see.

"Yes, darling, I hope you like them."

"Like them? Oh, I love them. I've never seen anything so pretty." She played with the jewels hanging from the straps, and he glanced over her head at Livia.

Livia mouthed, "Thank you," and all he could do was grin. This was the life he wanted—loving Livia, loving Cassia, and spending evenings together just being a family.

Livia tried to move and let out a low moan. Marius immediately jumped up to help her. Cassia moved her foot and scooted out of the way while Marius adjusted the pillows around Livia.

"I'm very tired," she said so only he could hear.

He nodded and said, "It's getting late. Let me help you turn on your side so you can rest."

With utmost care, he placed one hand behind her neck and one hand behind her knees and lifted her from a sitting position to a reclining one. Caecilia, who had been standing on duty in the corner, stepped to the opposite side of the bed and shifted the pillows. While he rolled her onto her side, Caecilia placed cushions behind her back and one in front of her so she could rest her arm on it. When Livia was settled, Marius turned to Cassia.

"How about we let your mother rest for the night? Come give her a kiss." He lifted Cassia so she could place a kiss on Livia's forehead without hurting her and then placed the child on the floor. He then also bent down and kissed Livia's forehead. "Until tomorrow, dearest one."

Livia's deep sigh and satisfied smile lightened his heart as he led Cassia from the room.

Chapter Seventeen

Over the next two weeks, a new routine developed in the Luciano household. Each morning, Marius visited Livia. He fed her a special broth the doctor recommended and made her drink herbal concoctions that were laced with medicine. He helped Caecilia dress each wound and helped Livia shift positions whenever she needed. The doctor usually came around mid-morning and assessed her wounds.

Cassia was allowed to enter the room after the doctor left each morning. She bounded in with her childlike energy and regaled her mother on all the happenings around the villa. Whenever Marius sensed Livia was tired, he invented a fun escapade to remove Cassia from the room so Livia could rest.

Some days, he took Cassia to the seashore and walked alongside her as she gathered shells, or fed the birds, or dipped her toes into the waves. Other days, he took her into town to visit Brother Justin, Jaalah, and Ezra. Their friendship was important to him as well as to Cassia, and he always enjoyed those outings.

Other days, he entertained her at the villa. They sometimes picked flowers to take to Livia and Helena. Other times, he put her in the capable hands of Anna and Fabia and watched as they transformed her into the little lady of the estate. And his most pleasant times came when they planned a feast to celebrate when Livia was healthy enough to leave her room.

After spending several hours with Cassia each day, he met with his mother. Helena was still cold toward him; but he had apologized for his outburst, and there was a new normal between them. Helena even sometimes snuck into Livia's room whenever Livia was sleeping. Helena would sit by the bed and watch. Caecilia informed Marius that Helena always left the room when Livia began to rouse. But the fact that she willingly went to Livia's room gave Marius hope.

Marius took his mother into town whenever he went to their emporium offices. He included her in their family business affairs and gave her the task of organizing and displaying their more cultured wares. He enjoyed working with her, and in those hours, Helena seemed happier and more fulfilled. They rarely discussed Christianity, but on occasion, she would randomly ask questions, mostly about his conversion. She wanted to know what had made him even consider Christianity. She wanted to know when he had rejected the gods of Rome. She wanted to know about the nobleman in Crete who had ultimately led him to Christ. The questions were never about the doctrines of his faith but more about his journey to it. Helena even began to join him and Cassia for dinner some evenings, and she promised to take part in the feast for Livia whenever Livia was ready.

Livia improved each day. Her wounds began to heal, and her strength began to return. Each evening after he settled Cassia into bed at night, Marius sat with Livia. Many times, she was asleep, and he watched her and prayed. In recent days, she was more alert, and they would talk. She wanted to hear all about his conversion. He gladly recounted his journey to faith and assured her that she was the one who made the difference in his soul's destiny.

He wanted to confess his love to her, but he bided his time, wanting the moment to be perfect. However, he continually used endearing terms for her, and he felt that she understood. She smiled each time he addressed her as precious, or darling, or dear one; and she didn't recoil when he kissed her forehead or hands. Even though she never reciprocated those sentiments, he knew she cared for him. At least, he hoped she did.

Livia slowly opened her eyes and tried to shift in her bed. Caecilia immediately came to her aid. "Let me help you, mistress."

Livia's brain still resisted the term *mistress*. Marius had explained her new position as a free Roman citizen many times, but she struggled to embrace the new role. Still, she thanked Caecilia and gladly accepted the help. The effort to move still left her a little breathless, but she recognized how much she had improved over the last couple of weeks. Crusty scabs replaced most of the oozing wounds on her body, and even though the scabs sometimes ripped open when she moved too much, overall, she was healing.

The gash in her arm was the most troublesome. The doctor believed it was broken and urged her not to use it. He did not have to convince her because she couldn't use it even if she tried. Any weight at all that she put on her arm still shot pain through her.

She glanced toward the window where the light of the sun filtered across her bed, and she wondered if she'd ever have the energy to enjoy the world outside her room again.

"Are you settled now, mistress?" Caecilia asked.

"Yes, thank you."

"Do you feel up for a visitor?"

Livia's eyes widened. "You mean, someone other than Master Marius or Cassia?"

"Yes, ma'am. Mistress Jaalah has been waiting for you to awaken."

Livia wanted to cry. "Yes, please send her in right away."

Within seconds, Jaalah was next to the bed, and the two women were sobbing and laughing all at once. "I would hug you if I had any idea how to do it without hurting you," Jaalah confessed.

Livia laughed. "I'd take one of your hugs, no matter how much it hurts."

But Jaalah simply patted her shoulder. "I won't be the cause of any more pain." She smiled at her friend and then pulled a chair close to the bed. Once she was sitting, she reached for Livia's hand and held it tightly while the women talked.

"How is Clio?" Livia asked, desperately wanting to hear good news.

"Oh, Livia, don't you worry at all about Clio. Master Marius has arranged for her care, just like he has yours, and she is doing really well."

Livia relaxed. "I'm so glad to hear that. Thank you."

For the first time since her release from prison, Livia felt safe to pour her heart out completely to her dearest friend. She cried a lot. She told Jaalah more details about her ordeal. She wept when she related the indignity of the flogging. She talked about the horrors of the prison. She talked about sensing God's presence every moment and having peace knowing her time had come. And then, she tried to explain how uncomfortable she was as a free Roman citizen.

"Two weeks ago, I was a slave sitting in a dank prison waiting for my execution. I was ready to go to Heaven. I was at peace. Now, I'm a free Roman citizen living in the greatest villa this side of Bythinia, and I don't know how to take it all in."

Jaalah patted her hand and listened.

"I know I should be grateful for Master Marius' generosity, but I'm just so confused."

"Is it your freedom that confuses you or Master Marius?" Jaalah asked.

Livia wanted to blame her emotional turmoil on her newfound citizenship, but she couldn't lie to Jaalah. "Oh Jaalah," she sobbed. "I don't understand my own heart. I don't know how to process anything anymore."

Jaalah stood and sat on the edge of the bed. "Do you love him, Livia?"

Livia whimpered. "Listen to yourself, Jaalah. You act like loving him is a possibility. It isn't. He is my master. He is Marius Luciano. He dines with the proconsul. He . . . " She closed her eyes and leaned her head back against the pillows. "I am nothing but a slave."

Jaalah grabbed her hand. "Livia, look at me."

Livia obeyed.

"We've talked about your feelings for Master Marius many times, haven't we?"

Livia nodded.

"I've always warned you to guard your heart with him. I've sensed your growing feelings for him for months, and as your friend, I've encouraged you to be careful."

Livia closed her eyes again. "I know, and I've tried."

Jaalah squeezed her hand. "But, Livia, we serve a God of miracles. He's the God Who parted the Red Sea. The wind and the sea obey Him. He's the God Who freed you from execution. And, Livia, He's the God Who loves us. Every gift we have is from above. And, Livia, I believe that God has miraculously given you a good and perfect gift in Master Marius."

Livia's eyes opened wide. "What are you saying?"

Jaalah laughed. "Livia, I'm saying this as your dear friend, but how can you not see how much Marius loves you? I know you think it isn't possible. But we serve the God of the impossible. He's orchestrated so many miracles in our lives. I think maybe He's working one more miracle for you and Marius."

Livia shook her head. "I . . . How can it be?"

"I'm going to ask you again, dearest friend. Do you love Marius?"

Livia cried, "I do. I'm afraid I've loved him for longer than I'm willing to admit. And Jaalah, if you could hear him talk. He's a different person completely."

Jaalah laughed. "Oh, believe me, you don't have to convince me of that. He spends many hours in our home drilling Justin with questions. You are right when you say he's a completely different person. He's been born again."

Livia smiled. "I don't know what this all means. It's new and uncertain, but the honest truth is, I love him. I do." She shrugged her shoulders and tilted her head. "I'm so confused by it all. And you are right. I think he cares for me, too."

Jaalah threw her head back and laughed. "You think?"

"Don't laugh. I don't know what to do about it."

"Oh, Livia, I don't think you need to do a thing. If I'm right about Marius, he'll help you figure it out when you get through all of your healing and are stronger. In the meantime, I suggest you take it one day at a time with him. Get to know the new Marius better. Just enjoy each moment and recognize it for the gift it is."

Livia took a long, deep, slow breath. "What will people say?"

"Those who love you will rejoice with you in all that God is doing in your life."

"Thank you, Jaalah. Thank you for coming and thank you for your friendship. I don't know what the future holds, but I am thankful that whatever comes, you are part of my story."

The two women talked for another hour until Livia's eyelids began to droop. Jaalah excused herself and promised to visit soon. After she left, Livia thanked God for Jaalah. "Lord, thank You for sending Jaalah to remind me of Your good and perfect gifts. And thank You for Marius. If he is part of Your plan for my future, then please show me clearly." She drifted into a peaceful slumber, and her dreams were sweet.

CHAPTER EIGHTEEN

In the days following Jaalah's visit, Marius noticed that Livia's energy seemed to increase. She wanted to try walking. With Marius and Caecilia on each side of her, she slowly walked around her room and, eventually, out into the hallway. Cassia led her to her own room and showed her all of the beautiful clothing, combs, jewelry, and furniture that now belonged to her.

Livia squeezed Marius's hand and whispered, "Thank you," each time Cassia showed a new favorite item. Marius noticed that Livia's eyes lingered on his longer and longer each time she thanked him. He felt his heart race with each gaze.

He led her back to her room and worked with Caecilia to position her comfortably on the bed. Cassia followed them and promptly plopped herself on the bed. "How did it feel to get out of this room for a while?" Marius asked.

"It was wonderful. Absolutely wonderful. And, Cassia, I can't believe how beautiful your room is."

"I love it, Mother. It's like a dream."

Livia smiled. "Yes, it is a dream," she replied to Cassia but directed her statement to Marius.

He smiled and covered her hand with his own. "It is all real, Livia. All of it."

She locked her eyes on his again, and he drank it in. He squeezed her hand and fought the urge to pour out his love for her, but Cassia interrupted.

"Your room is nice, too, Mother, but not as pretty as mine."

Livia laughed, and Marius took the opportunity to remove Cassia so Livia could rest.

"We have a lot of work to do, don't we Cassia?" He questioned the child. She grinned at her mother and jumped from the bed.

"We sure do."

Livia's eyes widened. "What are you two working on?"

"That, my dear, is a surprise," Marius replied.

While Cassia headed for the door, Marius stood. "I'll be back this evening." He lifted her hand and kissed her fingertips.

She sighed and smiled. "I look forward to it."

Caecilia offered some fruit to Livia, but she declined. "Caecilia, have I told you how grateful I am for you?"

Caecilia blushed as she placed the bowl of fruit on a cabinet. "Every day, Mistress."

"I'll never be able to repay your kindness to me. I'm sure I don't even know half of what you have done for me, especially those first few days I came home. Thank you."

Caecilia smiled and bowed. "It has been my pleasure to do what little I can to help you in your great suffering, Mistress." The slave busied herself with pouring some water into a goblet.

"At least drink something, Mistress."

Livia obeyed and took the goblet from the young maiden. She was just about to take a sip when she heard Helena's voice. "Leave us, Caecilia."

"Yes, my lady," the slave replied, and bowed low before exiting the room.

Livia's grip on the goblet tightened. She glanced at Helena and then looked away. She swallowed, but her mouth was so dry she had to clear her throat. She lifted the goblet to take a drink and splashed a few drops onto her tunica in the process. She fumbled trying to pat the excess water off her garment and wondered why she even bothered. In her clumsiness, she only spilled more. She could almost feel the sip of water sloshing down into her belly, and she suddenly felt queasy. She tried to shift her position, but with one hand on the goblet and the other arm still weak from injury, she couldn't budge.

"You can relax, Livia. I'm not here to distress you." Helena moved to the chair beside the bed and sat down.

"Yes, my lady," Livia replied.

Helena sighed. "You don't have to address me that way anymore, Livia. Haven't you heard? I'm no longer your mistress."

Livia glanced at Helena again. She sat perfectly straight in the chair with her hands folded in her lap. She held her head high and stared directly at Livia with unflinching resolve. While there was not an iciness to her demeanor, there certainly wasn't any warmth.

Livia wondered if she was expected to speak or if she should wait for Helena. The silence caused ominous thoughts to wriggle their way to the forefront of her mind, and Livia closed her eyes and gave her head a little shake. She took a slow, deep breath and opened her eyes again. Helena was still staring at her.

"Thank you for allowing Caecilia to care for me." Livia had no idea what to say, and that was the only thought that came to mind.

Helena rolled her eyes. "Of course," was all she replied.

Livia attempted another sip from her goblet and this time had more success. She took a long, slow drink and closed her eyes, hoping it would settle the uneasiness in her stomach; and after a couple of more sips, she felt calmer.

She turned to Helena again and waited. This time, Helena fidgeted. She broke her intense stare and reached for the chain around her wrist. With methodical precision, she passed it between her thumb and finger while shifting it around and around her wrist. Without looking back at Livia, she stated, "You've destroyed us. You know that don't you?"

Livia recoiled. Her mouth dropped open, and she felt tears stinging her eyes. Her head began shaking back and forth as Helena continued.

"Marius hates me because of you and your God. And even though he thinks we will be safe from scrutiny, our reputation will never recover once word gets out that he is a Christian. How could you do this to us?"

Livia leaned her head back against the pillow and wiped at her tears. Despite the harsh way in which Helena blamed her, Livia recognized Helena's argument was coming from a place of pain. Livia had a long history with Helena. She knew that the woman sitting next to her was once charitable and kindhearted. She knew the change in her character was a result of pain that gave way to bitterness. Suddenly, Livia wasn't uncomfortable with Helena. Instead, she was flooded with deep compassion for this woman who had suffered so much loss and heartache. Without fear, she lifted her head and spoke.

"My lady, I have loved you and your family the best way I know how. I would never intentionally cause you pain. Sharing my faith with Marius was an act of love, not animosity."

"You have no right to love Marius. No matter what legal papers he has signed, you are still a slave and so unworthy of him."

Livia was undeterred. "I know I am unworthy of him, Mistress. That is not the point. The point is that I try to love all people and I want more than anything for the people I love most to know the truth that can set them free."

"If you know you are unworthy of him, then why don't you just leave us when this is over and let us live in peace."

"Will that give you peace, Mistress? Am I the only thing that has robbed you of peace all these years?"

Helena's head jerked back to Livia. At first, her eyes narrowed in a stony rage, but Livia never flinched. Eventually, Helena's gaze changed. A weariness that Livia had not seen before overtook Helena's features. With a deep sigh, she whispered, "I've lost Marius. I've lost him." She dropped her gaze back to her hands and fiddled again with the chain on her wrists. For the first time, her stiff, straight shoulders drooped.

Livia wanted to grab Helena's hand and encourage her, but she could only speak. "Mistress, I've never asked you to do this in my entire life, but I'm asking you now. Will you look at me?"

Helena immediately lifted her head and stared at Livia. Her eyes were wide, and one eyebrow was raised.

Livia began slowly, "I was seventeen years old when your husband bought me and brought me to your estate. My parents had died, and I had no hope of a good life. I was terrified. The day that I arrived, Fabia took me to the servant quarters and scrubbed me from head to toe. I was humiliated. She gave me a new tunica and walked me through the villa showing me what would be expected of me. I cried almost the entire day. Fabia kept reassuring me that everything would be okay and that I didn't have to worry. She kept telling me that our mistress and master were good and kind."

Helena tilted her chin down and blinked rather quickly several times. She took a deep breath and then reset her shoulders as if bracing for a fight.

Livia continued, "That first day was one of the loneliest, most frightening days of my life up to that point. After working in the kitchen, I was supposed to go back to my quarters, but I couldn't remember how to get there. You came out of the triclinium, and the moment I saw you, I froze. I didn't know what to do or where to go or how to address you. I panicked so badly that to this day, when I think about it, I get anxious." Livia attempted to turn her body to face Helena more squarely, but she simply could not shift without help.

Instead, she simply continued with as much tenderness as she could emit through her words, "Mistress, that day, you told me how glad you were that I could join the Luciano household, and you asked me how I was settling in." Livia's voice softened as she relayed the memory.

"You laughed when I told you I couldn't remember where my quarters were, and you took my hand and walked with me all the way to the back of the villa. Your kindness to me that day was a balm to me then, and it continued to be a balm to me all these years. You were the one who encouraged me to marry Andrew, and you graciously served us a feast to celebrate our union. My life with him was beautiful, and you are the reason I enjoyed so many wonderful years with him.

"Mistress, I have loved you since the day I met you. And in these last few years where you have suffered such incredible loss and tragedy, I have tried to be a balm to you in the way that you were for me. I love you, Mistress. I'll always love you, and I'll always be grateful to you for the life you have given me. I don't want to bring more pain to you. I don't want to hurt you. I don't want to cause division between you and Master Marius." Livia's voice broke as she realized the impact of her words. If loving Marius hurt Mistress Helena, then how could she hurt this woman so deeply.

Helena didn't speak, but her eyes glistened.

Livia finished her impassioned plea with one final push. "Mistress, I don't know Master Marius's heart in most matters. But I do know two things. One, he loves you. He loves you more deeply today than I believe he's ever loved you before. He shows it in everything he does. You haven't lost him, Mistress. I believe you have actually found the real Marius. He is different than what you've known before because he has been born again. He's changed because he has met the one true and living God. He's at peace for the first time in his entire life; and the rift you feel isn't because he hates you, and it isn't because you've lost him. It is because he's a new creature."

Helena listened and nodded for Livia to continue. "The second thing I know is that the God Marius now serves loves you more than you can fathom. God wants to make you a new creature, too, Mistress. He wants to give you peace and rest."

Helena bristled. She rubbed her thighs, smoothing out the folds of her tunica, then rose. She stood next to the bed, and with a soft voice, she pleaded, "I'm asking you to leave us alone when you are better. Marius believes he's in love with you, and I have no doubt he wants to marry you. But I'm asking you to leave us in peace. I know he'll come to his senses when he's not so confused by the pity he has for you. It is pity, Livia, not love. He's just confused."

Helena's words stung. Livia turned away from Helena. A moment later, she noticed a momentary shadow flit across her bed as Helena exited the chamber. She pressed her head into the pillow and cried. *Please help us, Father.*

CHAPTER NINETEEN

Marius met Cassia in the hallway. They had decided it was time for Livia's feast. While Marius understood that Livia could never eat all of the rich foods that Cassia wanted to prepare, he also knew that the evening would be a special event to mark the miracles that God had wrought in their lives. "This is it, Cassia. Are you ready to get your mother?"

"I'm ready," Cassia replied, and they entered Livia's room.

Marius easily lifted her from the bed and carried her down to the triclinium. Helena had participated in decorating the room with flowers and pretty vases and had covered the table with her finest silver platters and porcelain dishes.

When everyone was seated, Marius clapped his hands, and servants began bringing tray after tray of scrumptious food. While Cassia sampled nearly every dish, Livia barely nibbled. Marius noticed that she did consistently sip her drink, and by the end of the evening, she had nearly finished two full goblets. Marius was satisfied that she had what she needed.

Marius hardly ate either. He was consumed with joy watching Cassia and Livia at his table. He had spared no expense, and when the meal was finished, his was the greater delight.

Throughout the meal, Cassia chatted between every bite. Marius and Livia spoke more through glances and smiles, and it was enough for Marius. He sensed her changing feelings for him, and he was satisfied.

Helena participated in conversation only when it was addressed directly to her. Marius could not help but compare Helena's detached demeanor at this feast with her lively personality at Pliny's feast. It pained him to see her so somber when his own heart was so full. The very cause of his happiness was the source of her distress. He was not surprised when she excused herself early for an evening stroll.

Although he would have enjoyed their company long into the night, he could sense that Livia was spent, so he offered to take her back to her chamber.

"Do you want to walk a little bit?" he asked.

"Yes, please," Livia replied.

Cassia, too excited to retire early, asked, "Master, when you said this was my home now and that I could move about freely, did you mean I could go into the gardens, too, even though no one is with me?"

"Of course. This is your home."

"And may I . . . may I pick some flowers, too?"

He smiled, knowing he would have a hard time ever refusing those dark eyes. "Yes, dear. You may choose whatever you want. But I wonder, don't you have enough flowers in your room? We've picked lots of colorful flowers this week, as many as would fill our vases."

"Oh yes, Master. My room is the prettiest place I've ever seen, but I wanted to pick something pretty for Mistress Helena. I know she is sad, and I want her to be happy."

Marius' voice cracked, so moved was he by her loving spirit. "I think that would be very lovely, Cassia. Perhaps Anna can fetch you a pretty vase for when you've made your final selection." He nodded toward the maid, and she bowed her acknowledgement and left to fulfill his command.

"Thank you, Master." Cassia rose, hugging his neck. He kissed her forehead, wanting to hold her forever, but she pulled away from him and went to her mother. "I'll come see you later. I know just which flowers Mistress likes. I can't wait to give them to her."

"I'm happy to see this change, my love. This is what will reach her." Livia's words were soft, but Marius still heard. Their affection stirred his heart even more.

"I finally understand. I really do, Mother. I'm so glad you are getting better. I thought you were going to die." Cassia sighed.

"But God used the governor to release you. I learned how God can even use an old, hairy pig to make things better; and if God wants to use me, He can. I want Mistress Helena to see God's love in me. I want her heart to change, too."

"What's this about a pig?" Mother laughed.

Cassia was already skipping toward the gardens. "I'll tell you all about it tonight, Mother."

Marius felt like an intruder to such an intimate moment. His heart ached with love for them, and he knew this was finally the right time to fully express his love and ask Livia to marry him.

Marius could see that the few steps Livia had taken on her own sapped her strength. Beads of perspiration covered her brow, and she was breathing heavily. Marius wondered how a woman so small and frail could have survived such an ordeal. She had come so far in her healing, but she was still weak. He offered his arm, and she leaned more heavily on him than he expected.

He led her slowly to the corridor and then quietly lifted her into his arms. Her weary body did not resist. When they reached her bedchamber, he lowered her to the bed. Caecilia placed the pillows at her back and helped her get more comfortable. Marius knew he could not wait another moment. It was unconventional, he knew; but tonight had been a celebration of Livia's healing, and it was the beginning of her new life.

"Livia, before I go, I . . . I must ask you something. Caecilia, please give us a moment."

"Yes, Master." The maid bowed and left the room.

For a moment, he felt unsure; but one glance at Livia and he found it easy to ask the question that had been burning in his heart for months. "Livia, I know that you have loved a man much greater than I. And I know that your heart still belongs to him in so many ways. But I would be honored if you would consider becoming my wife. I . . . I love you, Livia. I promise I will care for you and Cassia. I love her as if she were my own."

Livia studied his face, then dropped her eyes. "When you came to the prison and I learned of your salvation, I had joy greater than you could know. I had yearned to hear of it." She smiled deeply into his eyes. "I have prayed unceasingly for you since our conversations began in the garden two years ago, and the change in you is miraculous. But—"

"Shhh, don't answer now," he interrupted, unwilling to hear her objections. "Please, think about it more. I promise I will make you happy."

"Master—"

"Do not call me Master, for you no longer serve me. I am Marius."

"It isn't easy to change those roles—"

"I am willing, if you will let me. Oh, beloved, please don't turn me away."

She closed her eyes and sighed. His head dropped in despair, and he turned from her.

When his hand touched the door, she stopped him. "Marius."

His head jerked back, and his eyes were full of hope.

"I tried to guard my heart, and I did for a long time. But when you left on your last journey, I realized how much I missed you, and how often I thought of you, and how I longed to see you again. I should have guarded my heart more carefully, but I could never have seen what God had planned for me."

She stopped to swallow. Her voice was weak and hoarse, but she continued, "You are a good man. You have always treated everyone in your household well. You are ethical in business, and God has blessed you.

Furthermore, I have seen the love you have for Cassia, but I wonder."

She paused.

He crossed back to her side and grabbed her hand. "Yes, dear, what do you wonder about?"

"Is it really love that you feel? Could it be pity?" Her voice was so soft, he could barely decipher her words, but what she asked nearly broke him.

Marius shook his head vehemently. "Oh, Livia, how can you ask me that? I love you. I think you know that I do."

Livia's eyes welled with tears. "I can't deny that I love you, Master, but—"

"It's Marius, and that's all I've longed to hear," he interrupted.

"No, Marius. I need to finish." She wrangled her hand free from his and pushed him away. "How does your mother feel about your love for me?"

The hope in Marius's eyes faded. The expectation he felt was dashed, and he stepped away from the bed.

"It seems obvious to me that you already know how my mother feels."

Livia nodded.

"I have asked God to change her heart, and I don't want to hurt her. But, darling, I love you, and I love Cassia. Please say you will marry me."

Livia was quiet for many minutes. When she finally spoke, her voice was soft. "I cannot lie to you, Marius. I do love you. I can't think of anything I want more than to be your wife. But I can't marry you if doing so would push Mistress Helena further from God. I can't be responsible for hurting her more deeply than she's already been hurt. Please understand that."

"Oh, my beloved Livia, I feared you would reject me. Just knowing you love me . . . " He laughed and cried, drinking in the joy of this moment. Love filled him, rich and full, and his merry heart rejoiced. He knelt beside her bed and grabbed her hand again.

"I need to say this. I love you, Livia. It is not pity. I love you because together we have shared our grief, our hopes, and now our faith. I love you because God used you to open my eyes to the truth. I love you because you are the kindest, most loving woman I have ever known.

"I can see you are tired, darling. I suppose this wasn't the most romantic time to propose to you, but I am so glad. Knowing you love me has made me deliriously happy. I promise you this: I will not push our marriage again until my mother gives her willing consent. I love her more than I can say, and I want her to come to Christ more than anything. But I also want you to know that I believe God is changing her. I believe it is just a matter of time before she surrenders to Him. If she gives her consent, will you marry me?"

Livia reached her hand for his. "I will."

He bowed his head against their hands and wept unashamedly. "Thank you, darling. I love you so much."

He longed to spend the rest of the evening with his beloved, but her drooping shoulders and occasional grimaces led him to take his leave. He bent low and kissed her forehead gently. "Tonight, you rest. We have some praying to do. God loves my mother more than either one of us does. I believe that she will surrender to Him very soon. Then, we can rejoice together, and we can all begin a new future."

He nearly skipped to his room; and as he readied for bed, he reached into his leather pouch to retrieve a gift—a beautiful ring he had purchased long ago to give to Livia if she said yes. He hadn't opened the bag since the day he had left the prison, but he noticed the unopened scroll from Pliny that the guard at the prison had tucked into his pouch just as he had left the prison that day. Assuming it was some formal document authorizing the release of the prisoners, he broke the seal and unrolled the scroll.

As soon as he did, he dropped to his knees, falling prostrate before God. He cried out his praise for the great mercy of his Savior. For in his hands, he held the booklet listing the names of the known Christians in Nicomedia. Written at the bottom scrawled in the governor's own hand, was the name *Marius Luciano*, and scribbled hastily next to it were the words, "Pardoned all."

CHAPTER TWENTY

Helena sat on the marble bench staring at the statue of Apollo. The moonlight cast a soft hue, creating a calming glow around the stark white sculptures around her. She listened to the fountains as they bubbled over with soothing waters and envied their peaceful journey. She remembered the excitement her husband had felt when he brought in the engineers to construct the beautiful fountains. She had no idea how they managed to pipe the water in from the aqueducts with such pressure, but she had always cherished the moments she spent with her husband as he tried to explain it to her. He would walk her through each step of their estate as the builders worked to create their beautiful home. She would gladly give it all up if she could just see her dear husband again. How she missed him!

She hated the night. When the house quieted, she became restless. That's when the questions filled her mind. Her life seemed so futile, her accomplishments empty. She was wealthy, comfortable, and well-established as a noble woman in high Roman society. Her son was home and would be with her the rest of her life—however long that would be. And even though their relationship was strained, Marius was there, and she loved him. Nevertheless, despair had consumed her, and it showed on her fatigued face.

Have I been wrong all these years? Maybe what they say is true. Maybe it was my unbelief in the one true God that caused Him to take Gaius and Aurelia and my sweet Julia.

She studied the statue again, and it struck her that it was made of marble, just like the bench upon which she sat—just like the pillars around the garden, just like the bowls of the fountain.

"You are nothing but stone. You always have been, and you always will be—and I have been a fool."

Her thoughts raged within her. She faced the truth that she had long ago lost faith in the gods. She cringed, remembering all the offerings she had sacrificed begging for healing. When the physicians had failed her with their emetics, bloodletting, and purges, she had gone to the priests and paid homage at the temples. As she thought of the many treatments she had tried, all of which had failed, she remembered the only time she had ever experienced relief.

It was after the bloodletting, and she had been so weakened from the gruesome purge that she had prepared for death. The physician had even told the servants that her time had come. That night, as she lay ashen from the treatments, Livia had entered her chamber. She had knelt beside the bed, laid her hands across Helena's hands, and then prayed. Helena could not remember any of the words, but she remembered the sense of calm that had claimed her spirit that night. She remembered an almost immediate cessation of pain, and she remembered the unmistakable devotion in Livia's eyes.

A pink flush of color exploded onto her cheeks as she faced the shame of her behavior. Livia had shown her more love and affection than any other soul. She had tended to her with grace every evening, gently massaging her weary body, singing sweet and unusual songs, and telling stories from a book—a holy book, a Christian book. Helena knew what they were, but she had allowed it because it soothed her spirit.

When the pain became too great, Helena had tried poppy and mandrake; but she did not want to spend her last days in such a haze, so she had turned to strong drink. Again, shame washed over her when she realized what that drink had led her to do.

Now, she sat thinking about her life. Each day, she saw a little more of it slip away, and she was frightened. What if the words of Livia's book were true? What if Marius was right? What if this Jesus could give her the peace she so desperately longed for?

Her temples throbbed, and her neck was stiff. She rolled her head side to side, then let it hang while she rubbed the muscles behind her ears. Julia's necklace, hanging from her wrist, tickled her lobe. She looked at it, considering each link, wondering, *If God took her because of my unbelief, will He give her back to me if I follow Him?*

No. She shook her head. He was not the kind of God Who bargains and makes deals. But could this God be all that Marius claimed? Could He really bring hope?

If Marius, whose god had been nothing more than a quest for wealth and status, could experience such obvious change and if that new belief was so profound it would cause him to risk not only his status, but his life, then perhaps it was real. Marius. A new softness radiated from deep within him. He had found peace. Perhaps he was right, and it was time for her to surrender all the pain of her heart, the trouble in her spirit, and the sorrow in her soul. Perhaps it was time to shift her prayers from the stone gods of Rome to the unseen God of her slave. Perhaps—

A sudden movement at the far side of the garden caught her eye. Her eyes flickered, and she shrank away, not wanting to be disturbed. Her fists tightened, and the rage at being disturbed when she was so deep in thought quickly rose to the surface.

"Who is there?" she hissed into the darkness. "Show yourself at once."

Cassia obediently moved into the moonlight and stood trembling. "It's me, my lady. I just wanted to give—"

Helena gasped. "Julia?" She rose, reaching for Cassia's face, and stroked her cheek.

Cassia was confused. "No, my lady, it is me—Cassia."

"Cassia? What do you mean?" Realization flooded her. She rubbed her eyes, shaking her head. This wasn't her Julia. This was an imposter trying to take her place in Marius' heart. This child represented everything she'd lost.

Well, he could dress her in clothes that should have been Julia's; and he could weave pearls in her hair and give her freedom, but she would never be worthy to be his child.

She was suddenly furious, and she struck Cassia across the face.

The blow knocked the child backward, and a gasp of pain escaped her lips. Helena rubbed her temples, trying to regain control of her turbulent emotions. She drew back, surveying the still-white face of the child, and a cold emptiness swept over her. She was suddenly filled with self-loathing and stunned into silence. For the first time, Helena felt remorse.

She bent over the child, watching her cower as if readying for another blow. "I didn't . . . I'm sorry. I won't strike you again." Still, Cassia did not move. Helena watched as innocent tears spilled down Cassia's puffy cheeks, and Helena choked with pain, knowing there was no excuse for what she had done.

"Why are you out here so late at night, anyway?" She reached down, wanting to help Cassia stand, but the girl cringed and began gathering the flowers strewn about her on the cobblestone path.

Through muffled sobs, she sniffed. "I . . . brought these for you. I know . . . how sad you have been . . . and I wanted . . . to make you . . . happy."

"Why? Why would you . . . do such a thing . . . after all . . . I've done to you?" Her words came in short bursts.

"Because I love you, Mistress."

"You *love* me?" Helena stared at the girl in disbelief. How could this child love her after all the beatings she had endured at her hand?

"Yes, Mistress. I love you because God loves you— and because He loves me."

Helena dropped to her knees, finally willing to surrender, and she grabbed Cassia, cradling her in her arms. "Oh, Cassia, my darling child. I'm so sorry. Please don't cry."

Helena's heart completely broke. Deep, wrenching sobs tore from her chest as she sat rocking the little girl. The walls of bitterness and sorrow that for years had robbed her of peace came crashing down, and in the darkness of that quiet garden, she poured her heart out to the one true God.

Cassia cried, too. "It's okay, Mistress. Everything will be okay. Don't cry, Mistress. Don't cry."

That night, Helena surrendered her heart to God, and Cassia, young as she was, showed her mistress how to place her faith and trust in Christ.

When Marius walked into the garden later that night, he watched in amazement as his mother removed a precious, tiny chain from her wrist and fastened it around Cassia's neck. Her words sang to his heart a celebration of God's mercy and love.

"This golden chain was meant for my dear grandchild, but you are more than my grandchild. You are my sister, and I give it to you now as a promise of my love for as long as I live. Wear it, and all who see it will know that you are no longer bound by the bonds of slavery but that you are free and protected by the bonds of our love."

CHAPTER TWENTY-ONE

Just as the heat of the summer gave way to the cooler days of early autumn, Marius and Livia wed. The day was perfectly cool, with a soft breeze rising from the shores in the distance. Livia's health, though not yet fully restored, was improving daily, thanks to the lavish attention she received in Marius' loving care. On this day, her cheeks were no longer pale but were rosy and full. And even though she now had the strength to stand, she willingly looped her arm in Marius' as he led her down the path through the atrium of the Luciano villa. Friends, including Sister Clio, gathered around and worshipped together with them as they said their vows to each other.

When Brother Justin stood before them, he placed their hands together and held them between his own. "My friends, the joining of these two lives is a beautiful picture of the mercy of God. He has freed Livia and our sister Clio from prison."

He turned toward Marius and continued, "And you, Master Marius, have been freed from the bonds of sin."

He briefly let go of their hands and motioned for Cassia. When she reached him, he placed her small hand into Marius' and patted her on the head. "And, Cassia, because of the work of God in the hearts of your mistress and master, you and your mother have been freed from the bonds of slavery."

Her rich brown eyes smiled up at Marius, and he squeezed her hand.

Justin motioned for Helena to rise, and when she approached him, his voice broke. "And, Mistress Helena," he said, as he placed one hand in Cassia's and the other in Livia's, creating a circle of the small family, "God has used the faith of this child to free your heart from the bondage of bitterness and sorrow to lead you into everlasting peace."

Then, placing all of their hands together, he laid across them a simple gold chain. It was the chain Helena had given to Cassia. It no longer marked the death of a child, but now, it represented the birth of new life.

As the tiny family circle stood at the front of the crowd with their hands clasped together, Justin prayed, "Our Father, thank You for the freedom we have in You. Thank You for the miracles You have done in this family. As they stand here this morning, arms linked together in a chain picturing the newfound freedom You have given them all, I ask that You help us remember our responsibility to spread Your love to others so that all can stand fast in the liberty wherein You have made us free. Amen."

Suggested Reading

Davis, William Stearns. *Readings in Ancient History*. Boston: Allyn & Bacon, 1913.

Edersheim, Alfred. *Sketches of Jewish Social Life*. Peabody: Hendrickson Publishers, Inc., 1994.

Gower, Ralph. *The New Manners and Customs of Bible Times*. Chicago: Moody Press, 1987.

Heffernan, Thomas J. *The Passion of Perpetua and Felicity*. Oxford University Press, 2012.

Houghton, S.M. *Sketches from Church History*. Edinburgh: The Banner of Truth Trust, 1980.

McManners, John, ed. *The Oxford History of Christianity*. Oxford: Oxford University Press, 2002.

Packer, James I., Tenney, C. Merrill, and William White, Jr., eds. *The World of the New Testament*. Nashville: Thomas Nelson Publishers, 1982.

Pliny the Younger. *The Letters of the Younger Pliny*. Betty Radice, trans. London: Penguin Books, 1969.

Rasmussen, Carl G. *Zondervan NIV Atlas of the Bible*. Grand Rapids: Regency Reference Library, Zondervan Publishing House, 1989.

Schaff, Philip. *History of the Christian Church*. Peabody: Hendrickson Publishers, Inc., 2006.

ABOUT THE AUTHOR

Shawn D. Smith's passion for history has spurred her to use her vivid imagination to introduce readers to inspiring "friends" from the past. As she wanders through history, Shawn creates exciting stories surrounding historical events. In her blog, she also scribbles her take on the men and women who have bequeathed their rich legacies of faith to us. Shawn, her husband Dave, and their three daughters spent fourteen years as missionaries to Papua New Guinea. For more than a decade of that time, they lived in the primitive Simbai tribe. Then they served fourteen more years in the leadership of their mission before returning to serve in Asia, where they reside today. Shawn is an experienced homeschool mom, regular Bible study teacher, and popular conference speaker. With a bachelor's degree in history and master's degrees in Education and in Library and Information Science, she is fulfilling her dream of encouraging others by teaching history through her stories. She blogs about her favorite heroes at scribblesbyshawn.com.

For more information about
Shawn D. Smith
&
The Freedom Chain
please visit:

www.scribblesbyshawn.com
www.facebook.com/ScribblesbyShawn
IG: @scribblesbyshawn

Ambassador International's mission is to magnify the Lord Jesus Christ and promote His Gospel through the written word.

We believe through the publication of Christian literature, Jesus Christ and His Word will be exalted, believers will be strengthened in their walk with Him, and the lost will be directed to Jesus Christ as the only way of salvation.

For more information about
AMBASSADOR INTERNATIONAL
please visit:

www.ambassador-international.com
@AmbassadorIntl
www.facebook.com/AmbassadorIntl

To help further our mission, please consider leaving us—or ask your parents to leave us—a review on social media, your favorite retailer's website, Goodreads or Bookbub, or our website, and be sure to check out some of our other books!

When Luke Alexander's father is "missing, presumed dead," Luke and his friends decide to start a search of their own. Little do they know that their search will take them on the wildest adventures of their lives and make the stories of Solomon's temple and other biblical events seem more real than they ever thought possible. Will their adventures lead them to Luke's father, or will they only wind up with more questions than answers?

The Heart Changer is a delightful telling of the Old Testament story of Naaman, captain of the Syrian army, and how he was cured from leprosy. Miriam, the unnamed Israelite slave girl of the Bible, tells the story of her captivity, of her role in the captain's healing, and of her own heart's redemption.

Melanie Cooper's life seems perfect. She's the star on her swim team, she has great friends, and she's turning thirteen in just a few weeks. But when her family is forced to move to Northern California, her world starts to unravel. Can Melanie learn to trust in a God that allows bad things to happen? Discover with Melanie how He can bring something good even from the difficulties in our lives.